Take a Chance on Me

TAKE A CHANCE ON ME

A Love on Chance Avenue Romance

JANE PORTER

TULE
PUBLISHING

DEDICATION

For all the book girls everywhere—
We really should rule the world!

CHAPTER ONE

I T WASN'T OFTEN that she had a stranger in her chair at The Wright Salon, much less a thirty-something-year-old male, that also happened to be ruggedly handsome, as in the handsome of the inscrutable romance cover hero.

Amanda Wright knew her romance cover heroes, too, as she and her sister Charity had lived off them growing up, surviving their harsh reality by living on fantasies and fairy tales. Jenny, their oldest sister, had been appalled, and would confiscate their paperbacks, tossing them out if she found them. Which was why Amanda and Charity learned to hide their romances between their mattresses, or stuff them inside the sleeves of their ugly, thrift store rainbow-hued winter coats.

Romance cover heroes were usually darkly handsome as well as brooding and enigmatic, traits found perhaps in the Highlands or Mediterranean principalities, but not in most small Montana towns. No, in small Montana towns like Marietta, men tended to be polite, practical, and dependable, and there was nothing wrong with practical and dependable men, but it just wasn't exciting, and Amanda was holding out for a true romance hero, one that wasn't just handsome, but a man that was powerful, successful, complex. *Enigmatic.*

And her client, Ty James, could easily pass for the enigmatic romance hero with his thick brown hair, light eyes the color of the sea, chiseled jaw, and firm chin. Never mind his lips which were pretty much perfect, especially when he smiled, which he didn't do a lot. But when he did, it was the smile of movie stars—confident, easy, sexy—which made it almost impossible to focus, which wasn't a good thing as she was wielding very sharp scissors, very close to his strong, tanned nape. True, he had what romance novels called a Roman nose, which meant it wasn't small and straight, but a little bit prominent, but that just made his features all the more interesting. Amanda liked a good nose on a man, it kept him from being too pretty, and a nose with a hook or bump at the bridge implied he'd had it broken, maybe in a fistfight, maybe through sports. Either way, it was manly. Masculine.

"You've been a stylist for a long time?" he asked, as she gently pressed his head forward a bit, trying to give her a better view of his hairline while also trying to hide his gorgeous reflection from her line of sight. His masculine good looks were distracting. *He* was distracting, and she didn't normally fall for just every handsome face. In fact, she couldn't remember the last time a man made her heart pitter-pat, and it wasn't just doing a pitter-pat right now, but a full-on, racing horse gallop.

"Nine years," she answered, "six full-time. The first three I was in college."

"You did both?"

"I needed a job and it turned out I was good at it."

"Where did you go to college?"

"I stayed local. Montana State, in Bozeman."

"And what did you study?"

"Psychology." She paused, ran her comb through the back of his hair, checking the length, making sure lines were straight. She glanced up into the mirror, caught his eye, and noted his surprise. She shrugged, lips curving. "I like people."

"You must get to know your customers quite well."

"I do. I'm very attached to my customers." She paused, smiled again, a little more ruefully. "Well, most of them. There are a couple that drive me slightly bonkers, but they just make me appreciate the rest all the more."

"What do the frustrating ones do to drive you bonkers?"

"Arrive thirty minutes late for a forty-five minute appointment, or forget to show at all."

"That's it?"

She smiled again, and shrugged. "I have really good customers."

His green gaze held hers in the mirror and for a moment she completely lost focus.

"I noticed you had more starred reviews on Yelp than any other stylist in town," he said, snapping her attention back.

"I do encourage them to leave a review if they're happy," she answered.

"Clearly, they're happy."

"It's a win-win, then." Amanda felt herself growing warmer by the moment.

What on earth was wrong with her? Hand shaking, she reached for her colorful bottle on her station shelf and took a quick drink of water, trying to cool herself off. It had obviously been far too long since she'd spent time with an attractive man because this was ridiculous. She was genuinely flustered.

"You have a name on the back of one of your chairs," he said, watching her in the mirror. "Is it a memorial?"

She looked to see where he was pointing and laughed. "Oh, no. No! Bette is very much alive, as well as a very dear client and friend. She did something nice for me and so I gave her her very own chair. Only Bette is allowed to sit there, and that way she always knows I have time—and a spot—for her."

"She must have liked that."

"I think so." Mandy took a comb and drew it through his hair, checking the length. "So you're in town for a meeting tomorrow?"

"Yes."

"And you're staying at the Graff?"

"It's a nice hotel."

"I've never actually stayed there, but it's fun to go for drinks or their Sunday brunch."

"Do you go often?"

"A couple times a year. Just for special occasions. Most of the time my sister and friends head to Grey's. More our style, as well as a lot less spendy."

TYLER JAMES JUSTICE had expected Amanda Wright to be polished and stylish—she did hair for a living, after all—but he hadn't expected her to be quite so pretty.

Or kind.

Or appealing.

But she was pretty, strikingly pretty, and disarmingly sweet. Make that charming. For a moment he'd wondered if she'd had work done, and then he spotted the photo of three gorgeous blonde women tucked into her mirror, their faces close, arms wrapped around each other, and they were all beautiful. "Girlfriends or sisters?" he asked, nodding to the photo.

She steadied his head, preventing him from moving again. "Sisters. I'm the baby."

"When was this picture taken?"

"My sister's wedding a couple years ago."

"Do your sisters live here in Marietta, too?"

"Charity does. Jenny and her husband have a ranch in Colorado."

"What does Charity do?"

Mandy didn't answer immediately, her elegantly arched brows flattening as she concentrated on trimming the hair close to the tip of his right ear. On one hand he was impatient for her to answer, but on the other he appreciated her attention to detail and not nicking his ear.

"She works as the receptionist for a Realtor on Main Street," Amanda finally said, before tipping his head forward and taking a razor to his nape, cleaning up the back of his neck. "I'm hoping, though, to eventually bring her here to help me manage the salon."

"It wouldn't be hard working with her?"

"Not at all. Charity is my best friend. We're two peas in a pod. Mom used to say we were more like twins than twins. What about you?" she asked. "Do you have brothers or sisters?"

He hesitated. "I had a brother. He died serving the country."

HER HAND WENT to his shoulder, her touch firm, warm. "I'm sorry," she said quietly.

He swallowed around the unexpected lump in his throat. He rarely talked about Coby, and he never got emotional when he did, and he wasn't at all sure why he'd mentioned his brother to her, and he certainly didn't want to continue with such a personal conversation. He hadn't come here to

Marietta to be anyone's friend. He was worried about his grandmother, and in particular, this young woman's influence over his grandmother. It was a difficult time to be away from work, too, but when he'd heard his grandmother was considering amending her will to leave her house to Amanda 'Mandy' Wright, he knew he had to come and sort things out.

"I couldn't imagine losing one of my sisters," Amanda said after a moment. "It must have devastated your parents."

He nodded, unable to say more, because it had devastated them, and Coby's death had changed the dynamics of the family, not that their family had ever been the perfect family. His father and grandfather had no relationship, which meant Tyler really never knew his grandfather, either. His grandmother, Bette, was another matter. His grandmother was sweetness and light... the kind of grandmother that deserved those silly mugs that read World's Best Grandmother.

"You said you were here for business," the stylist added, thankfully changing the subject. "You must be in the ranching business then."

"No. I'm in tech."

Her full lips pursed. "Tech?"

"I design games."

"Games?" she repeated, a delicate eyebrow arching.

"Computer games."

"That must be fun." Her eyes met his in the mirror. She was smiling and her smile did something funny to his chest.

"It's creative," he answered.

"You're giving people something fun to do. Good for you. People need entertainment to help us unplug from the world, don't you think?"

He found himself watching her as she took the big soft brush and went over his nape, brushing off stray hair. He hated being so cynical, but was she for real? "I do."

"I've never played games, but I love to read, and go to the movies. Feel-good movies. I avoid the depressing ones."

He wished he'd been prepared for her, and not just how pretty she was with her high cheekbones and gleaming blonde hair pulled back in a high teased ponytail, but her kindness and good nature. She reminded him of spring rain—sweet and refreshing—which wasn't at all his impression of her before he came.

"How is the length?" she asked, turning the chair and handing him a mirror so he could see the back of his head. "Any shorter?"

"It's a little longer than I usually wear it," Tyler said. "But I like it. Looks good."

"I think so, too. It gives you a '70s rock star vibe."

He felt a strange rumble of laughter in his chest, strange because he didn't really laugh much, not anymore. His world had become so weighty and serious. "I'm far from that."

"I don't know." A dimple appeared at the corner of her full lips. "If you're a game designer, you can be anyone you want to be." She unsnapped the black plastic cape, removing it from around his shoulders. "How long are you in town?"

"Through the weekend."

"Well, I hope you enjoy your stay. Marietta is a great little town. Everyone that comes here, falls in love—"

"Don't say that."

"With the town," she finished, laughing again. "But what's wrong with falling in love?"

"Nothing. But I'm not looking for love. Or a new place to live. I like Austin."

"A Texas boy."

California, he wanted to correct her, as he'd only relocated to Austin two years ago, but there was no point in telling her any of that. They weren't friends, and furthermore, once she knew who he really was, they'd never be friends. The warmth inside of him cooled, and his faint smile faded. Standing, he reached for his wallet. "How much do I owe you?"

"Thirty-five. And you can pay Emily. She's at the desk in reception."

"You did a good job."

"Then leave a review," she teased, reaching for the broom and dustpan tucked in the corner next to her station. "And enjoy Marietta. It's a great place to be."

"I'll try," he answered.

"Not good enough," she called after him.

He turned in the doorway to look back at her, all golden blonde and astonishingly pretty in the winter sunlight, and yet she was smiling at him in a way that made his chest ache.

She made him feel young and hopeful, just as he'd felt as a boy when he'd see a cute girl. But he wasn't a boy, and he wasn't in town because he wanted to be, but because he needed to be. He'd arrived to put distance between this woman and his grandmother, a move that wasn't going to make him popular with anyone, but he was a man who did what needed to be done. That was what had made him who he was today. "Good-bye."

"Good luck tomorrow."

TYLER FELT STRANGELY out of sorts as he left the salon on Church Avenue and walked to his car. A few patches of dirty snow still dotted some of the neighboring lawns, but otherwise the streets and sidewalks were clear. In the distance he could see the peak of Copper Mountain rising behind the small Montana town. So far, he didn't love or hate Marietta. It was just a small town in the middle of nowhere and not easy to reach. He'd taken two flights to get here from Austin, flying Austin to Denver, and Denver to Bozeman, and then he'd needed a rental car to drive the thirty-five miles from Bozeman to Marietta. Not impossible, just by no means convenient, particularly when there were power struggles internally at TexTron. He'd survive the power struggles, but it would be less stressful weathering storms if he were in the office than here in remote Crawford County, Montana.

As he crossed the street, he wondered what his grandmother, Bette Justice, would think when she found out he'd booked an appointment with her favorite stylist, Amanda Wright, a young woman she claimed was one of her best friends, and so important to her that in the past few years she'd given her a large financial gift, and was now wanting to leave the young woman her house on Bramble.

Tyler was a self-made man. He didn't need his grandmother's money. But at the same time, he wanted to be sure his grandmother wasn't being unduly influenced, or pressured in any way. Gram had been on her own for almost seven years now, and it was probably too much isolation from her family, so he wasn't entirely surprised that she'd come to depend on outsiders, which was why he was here now. He'd wanted her to move in with him for years, and he'd been trying to convince her that the move would be good for both of them, because he wanted to take care of her. But he couldn't do that with her in Montana while he was in Austin.

He'd arrived today in Marietta thinking the worst of Amanda Wright, but after thirty minutes in her chair, he discovered she was nice, and rather charming, and he could see why Gram was fond of her. But there was a difference between being fond of someone and giving them sizeable financial gifts… or a sizable chunk of her estate.

Gram's announcement that she would soon amend her will got his attention and he cleared his schedule at work, booked the flights, and now here he was, in his father's hometown, a town his father absolutely hated.

BETTE JUSTICE ARRIVED at The Wright Salon twenty minutes early for her two o'clock appointment because she'd come bearing gifts—two chicken salads from Java Café.

"Emily said you had a short break between appointments," Bette said as Amanda appeared at the receptionist desk. "So we're going to eat first."

"What if I already ate?" Amanda answered, smiling indulgently.

"But you haven't. Emily said so."

Amanda shot her receptionist an amused glance before leading Bette to the white painted table in the corner of what once had been the dining room but was now a mix of small round tables and comfortable seating for salon guests to use for meals and relaxing in between appointments.

"By the way, I have news," Bette said, opening their salads and arranging the place settings on the table.

"Oh?" Mandy replied, bringing two glasses of water to the table and sitting down opposite Bette.

"As you know, my grandson wants me to move to California. But he's getting serious now. He thinks I must move... that it's not good for me to be living alone."

"Why not?"

"He worries I might fall or have an accident."

"He's been watching too much TV."

"Agreed. But he's now taking action. He's arriving this weekend. He's determined to get me to move—"

"But he can't force you!"

"No. He can't. But I don't want to alienate him, either. I appreciate that he's concerned about me. He's the only family I have left, but I don't want to live in San Jose or Saratoga or wherever he's calling home now." She poked her salad with her fork but didn't even try to eat. "Marietta is my home. It's always been my home. It's where I raised my family and all my friends live—" She broke off and blinked back tears. "I wish I could make him understand, but he truly believes I will be better off with him in California than Montana."

Amanda frowned. Bette was one of the sunniest, most cheerful women she knew, and it was hard to see her like this. "It's going to be okay," she said, covering Bette's hand with hers. "He isn't even here yet, and when he does arrive, you'll just have to show him why you love Marietta so much so that he understands why you're happy here."

"I am torn, though. I would love to be closer to my grandson. He reminds me so much of my son. And I suppose that's both good and bad, because Tyler's father, Patrick, was really my heart. I had such difficulty conceiving, and had five miscarriages. Patrick was really my miracle baby. We'd given up thinking I could have a child, and then I was pregnant and he somehow made it all the way through, and so of course I was protective of him. Don, my husband, thought I spoiled him, but how could I not? Patrick was a joy... smart, busy, gregarious. He had the most delightful sense of humor and loved to make people laugh. Unfortunately, Don didn't have a sense of humor and, from the beginning, he and Patrick butted heads. It didn't help that Patrick was extremely independent, and he wanted to do things his way."

"But isn't that normal? Kids rebel. It's part of growing up."

"They do, yes, absolutely, but my late husband was a former military man, and he expected his son to follow orders. Only Patrick didn't follow anyone's orders, not unless they made sense to him, and the more Donald tried to discipline Patrick, the more Patrick resented his father. And then they had a huge fight over a girl Patrick was dating. Donald didn't approve of her, and Patrick was told that we wouldn't help him with college if he didn't stop seeing her. Patrick didn't, and Donald threw him out, a month before his high school graduation."

"What happened then?"

"Patrick graduated, and left for the West Coast, where he went to school on an ROTC scholarship, and he came home only one more time, and then never again."

Bette sighed. "It was a mess, and heartbreaking."

"Especially if he was your only child."

"I was constantly in the middle of those two, and so it

was something of a relief when Patrick went away to school, but in some ways it was even worse when he never returned after that first visit."

"Did you not see him then?"

"I'd go see him in California, but Don wouldn't go with me."

"So you were always in the middle."

Bette's eyes filled with tears. "Patrick died a year after Don in a skiing accident. It was just one of those freaks accidents."

"I remember that."

Bette nodded. "And now I have this chance with my grandson, and while I don't want to leave Marietta, I don't want to risk losing out on this chance to know him better, and have him in my life."

"I completely understand that."

"He doesn't understand Montana, though. He thinks our winters are too long and harsh. He worries about me being here all alone."

"You can't blame him, not if he's a Californian. But you're also far from alone."

"I know, and that's why I want you to help me when he comes to visit this weekend. I want you to show him around Marietta. Give him a tour of the area... let him see the Marietta we know and love."

"Me?"

"You're young and pretty—"

"This is a very bad idea."

"He'll love you."

"I don't want him to love me. I want him to love you. And I want him to support your desire to remain in Marietta for as long as you wish to be here." Amanda's gaze met Bette's. "You do want to still be here, don't you? Or, are you maybe ready for a move to Northern California?"

"Marietta is home," Bette answered firmly. "This is where I want to be."

"You could always come back here for visits—"

"And leave all my friends? Leave my bridge group? And my birthday group? The girls and I have been together for over fifty years!"

Amanda smiled, because she knew Bette's bridge club and birthday club and the 'girls' were all in their eighties as well. "You do have great friends here."

"Exactly! I just need a little help convincing him that Marietta, Montana is where I belong."

Mandy gave Bette a long look. "Just know that I won't be part of your matchmaker schemes."

"I wouldn't!"

"You have. Several times."

"Well, I promised you I wouldn't interfere, and I haven't again, have I?"

"No. And that's good, because I've never been happier, nor have I ever worked harder. The last thing I want, or need, is a man. He'd only complicate everything—" She broke off, her brow creasing. "What *did* you say his name was?"

"Tyler Justice."

So not Ty James, Mandy thought. But just to be on the safe side, she had to ask. "Does he ever go by Ty? Or Ty James?"

"Well, his middle name is James, and I suppose people might call him Ty. His parents called him Tyler, and I've only ever called him Tyler." Bette paused. "Why do you ask?"

"Do you have a picture of him?"

"I do somewhere. Not here."

"Not on your iPhone?"

"I still don't know how to do that, Amanda."

Mandy hid her smile. "What does he look like?"

"Why all these questions?"

"I'll tell you in a minute. Just humor me. Is he tall or short? Does he have dark hair or is he blond? Does he even have hair?"

"Of course he has hair! He has thick brown hair and green eyes, and he's a little over six feet tall. Maybe six feet one. And he's handsome. He has a lovely face—he inherited his dad's good looks. I know I'm his grandmother but Tyler is swoon worthy."

"Huh."

"Why?"

She pictured the tall, broad shouldered man in her chair

earlier, and the high hard cheekbones, as well as the firm chin and strong brow. "I was just curious. Just in case I... bump... into him here in town."

"He's not arriving until Friday night."

"And then he'll be staying at the Graff?"

"No! With me, of course." Bette looked indignant. "I'd never let family say at a hotel. That's dreadful."

"Right."

CHAPTER TWO

H ER THREE O'CLOCK appointment was a no-show due to car troubles, and Amanda was almost glad because her brain was spinning and her stomach was churning. After glancing at her watch, and then out the window, she grabbed her coat and told Emily she'd be back in time for her four o'clock client, and then buttoning her coat, Amanda headed down Second Avenue, toward Main Street and then on to Front before turning to the Graff.

It was a cloudless day, just cold and windy, not surprising as it was late February and Marietta was always windy. Amanda walked briskly, the odd leaf and twig swirling past, taking deep breaths, trying to check her temper, but it wasn't easy because she was seriously angry. She'd been played by Bette's grandson, no less.

Amanda asked the front desk if there was a housephone she could use to call Tyler James's room. The rather dour front-desk clerk pointed to the phone against the lobby wall, but then added, "But he's not in his room at the moment. He was just here asking about a place to get food and I directed him to the bar."

Amanda nodded her thanks and headed to the back where the old-fashioned bar had a cozy pub feel with its green leather booths, big antique counter, and glowing copper ceiling. After being refurbished for much of the last year, the handsome, antique bar was back in place, in its position of glory, and Amanda's friend, bartender Shane Knight was behind the counter.

Amanda nodded at Shane and then scanned the room, spotting Tyler at a booth on the opposite wall.

Her temper spiked again. "Tyler James Justice," she said, reaching his side.

He'd been reading a message on his phone and his head lifted abruptly. As his gaze met hers, his expression went from pleased to surprised and then wary.

"Your grandmother thinks you're arriving Friday night," she added tersely. "Won't she be surprised when she discovers you actually arrived on Tuesday and have been staying at the Graff."

"Care to sit?" he replied, gesturing to the leather booth across from him.

She looked at him for a long moment before sliding into the booth.

"When did you figure out I was her grandson?" he asked.

"When she came by at lunch and told me her grandson, Tyler Justice, was coming to town and she hoped I'd be nice to you and show you around." Amanda smiled grimly. "It wasn't difficult to put Ty James and Tyler Justice together."

"You haven't told her I'm here though, have you?"

"No. I don't want to upset her. She's excited about your visit. She's so looking forward to seeing you." She continued to hold his gaze, wanting him to feel the full weight of her displeasure. "I'm not entirely sure why you told her Friday and arrived Tuesday, but that's none of my business. I just don't want to see her hurt."

"And why would I hurt her?"

"I'm not sure. But maybe sneaking into town—"

"I'm not sneaking."

"She doesn't know you're here though, and you gave me a false name."

"I gave you my name."

"But not your surname. Because you knew I'd recognize the name Justice." Her voice grew harder, her tone frostier. "Not sure what you were doing in my chair earlier, asking so many questions."

"She's talked a lot about you. I was curious to find out more about you."

"Then why not introduce yourself as Bette's grandson? You commented on her chair. You heard me say she was a favorite client."

The waitress approached, and asked if Amanda would like to order something. Amanda was about to say no, when she realized she was shivering on the inside, from nerves and cold. "I could use a coffee."

"Nothing to eat?" Tyler asked.

"No, but thank you," she added to the waitress, giving her a smile. Her smile disappeared as the waitress walked away and she looked at Tyler. "I'm not hungry because I had lunch with your grandmother an hour ago, just before her hair appointment."

"Do you do that often?"

"Once or twice a week."

"Is she that lonely?"

Amanda stiffened. "What kind of question is that?"

"I'm genuinely curious."

"Your grandmother is not at all lonely. She plays in a duplicate bridge group. She is part of a birthday club. She is part of a gardening club. Bette organizes a weekly movie matinee day at the Palace Theatre and she is the ringleader of thirty some seniors that meet for the movies every Wednesday. Why don't you go tomorrow and see how lonely she is?"

"Why so hostile?"

"Why assume she is lonely, just because she and I are close?"

His broad shoulders shifted carelessly. His expression was equally detached. Amanda couldn't get a read on him.

"I would think you'd both prefer the company of someone closer to your own ages," he said.

Her chin notched up. "Apparently, you're confused, but then, you're not the only one. Bette is confused, too. She thinks you're arriving Friday to convince her to move to California, only you're not living in California, are you?

Didn't you say you're in Austin? Maybe you should explain to her where she'd live and why, since she thinks you're a stand-up, honest guy?" She gave him another long, pointed look before rising. "I'll get my coffee to go."

"I am an honest guy. And if you'd give me a chance to explain—"

"I don't believe in manipulating people or playing games."

"I'm not playing games."

"That's right. You just design them." She shot him a re-proachful look and started for the bar counter but he reached out to catch her sleeve, his fingertips just brushing the inside of her bare wrist.

"What are you going to tell my grandmother?" he asked.

It had only been the briefest of touches, and yet she could still feel the warmth of his skin against hers, and for a moment she couldn't think, torn between anger and disap-pointment. She'd so enjoyed talking to him earlier, when she'd cut his hair, and yet now she just wanted to put distance between them. "I'm not going to tell her anything. She's your grandmother. But do the right thing so that you don't end up hurting her. She's so excited to see you. Be kind to her."

"I would never hurt her. I adore Gram—"

"Well, so do I." And then she moved on, walking to the bar where Shane was pouring drinks.

"What can I get for you, Mandy?" Shane asked, brushing

a long tendril of blonde hair behind her ear.

"I'd ordered a coffee but I need to get back to the salon. Can I get it to go instead?"

"No problem."

Shane filled a paper cup, popped a lid on it, and handed it over, but then waved off Mandy's money. "I've got this. Get back to work and keep making Marietta beautiful."

Amanda laughed and headed out, but her smile faded as she approached Tyler's booth. She squared her shoulders, and kept her gaze fixed on the door so she wouldn't make eye contact with him, and then only exhaled after she was in the hall.

FOR A MOMENT Tyler just sat there, watching Amanda exit the hotel bar, and then he rose and threw down some bills and followed her out.

Amanda was hurt, and angry, and he didn't blame her. He should have told her who he was earlier, especially when his grandmother's name was mentioned, but he wanted to learn as much about Amanda Wright as he could, without her being guarded, or defensive, but of course she didn't know any of that.

He caught up with her in the middle of the Graff's formal lobby. "Slow down," he said gruffly, putting a hand to her upper arm. "Please?"

She stopped walking to face him, but her expression was

no longer friendly or smiling, and it crossed his mind that while he still didn't know very much about her, he'd discovered that although pretty, she wasn't soft, and she wasn't a pushover. Amanda Wright had a backbone. Nor did she appreciate being played for a fool.

"I'm sorry," he said, his voice deep, and rough. He was uncomfortable and embarrassed. "I'm sorry I didn't tell you who I was earlier. And I apologize if I've made things awkward. That wasn't my intention."

"Then what was your intention, booking me for a haircut and giving me a false name?"

"It's my real name."

"And telling me you were here for a business meeting?" She looked him in the eye, unblinking, unflinching. "What was that about?"

"I do have a business meeting. Two, actually, one with an investment broker, and another with a local Realtor."

"Why? Are you investing in Marietta? Thinking of a buying a house, or business here?"

"It never hurts to understand a local economy."

Her full lips compressed. "There are different ways to get to know a community. There is more to Marietta than its economy—which is booming, lately. If you really want to know why your grandmother loves Marietta, get to know her friends. Discover the town. Join her for the Wednesday matinee movie. Take her to dinner at Rocco's, or pie at the diner—"

"Gram turns eighty this year."

"That's right, in June, and we're working on a lovely party for her, too."

"She's not going to live forever."

"No one does, Ty. But what makes you think she'd be happier living with you in Texas or wherever it is you call home now?"

"Well, I'd be there."

"Yes, but you work, don't you? And I'm sure you have a social life. You're not going to sit home with her twenty-four seven."

"She'd make new friends."

Amanda drew a sharp breath, furious. "Of course you'd say that." Frustration filled her. He didn't get it, did he? Bette would be lost without her friends in Marietta. Her friends were the ones that had been there for her after Don's death, and Patrick's funeral. Friends had given her life meaning. They wouldn't be easily replaced. Nor would Marietta be the same without her. "You don't understand how important she is here in Marietta, and how much she does for the community."

"I know she's a generous source of support—"

"This isn't about her making donations and writing checks." Amanda gripped her cup tightly. She couldn't remember when she last felt so upset. "Bette is loved. And she loves us. And we don't want to lose her."

"Neither do I."

"Then start spending time here! Come see her. Get to know her on her terms. Don't make her sacrifice everything just to have a relationship with you."

"Life is about change. It's about being flexible, adaptable."

"You might be brilliant at creating software, but you don't know the first thing about people. She's not a character in one of your games. Maybe you're the one that needs to be flexible and adapt."

"What does that mean?"

"Maybe you should consider moving here." And then she was walking away from him again, quickly. This time he didn't pursue her.

TYLER WALKED FROM the Graff to his grandmother's house on Bramble. Her home was on the north end, closer to the high school than the courthouse. Many of the homes around her were modest Victorians, nothing as grand as the big, stately homes surrounding the historic Bramble House B&B but they all embodied turn of the century American charm.

It was a good fifteen minute walk and the wind blew hard the entire time, the blast cold and strong. He ran a hand through his hair. Amanda Wright had given him a good cut, but he wasn't sure what to think of her. She looked soft and pretty but she didn't pull punches, and ordinarily he appreciated straight talk—he was known for being a hard hitter himself—but he didn't need her lecturing him on his grandmother. Who was she to judge him? Furthermore, who was she to come between him and his grandmother?

He didn't want to move Gram, but he didn't have a choice. She was almost eighty and she wasn't as strong as she used to be. She needed her family around her. She needed to be looked after, and not by strangers. Once she moved to Austin he'd be there to keep an eye on her. He could have lunch with her and dinners with her. Their visits wouldn't be so painfully infrequent. He hated that it took multiple flights to get to his grandmother, requiring him to schedule visits weeks, if not months, in advance. Gram was special, and now that his dad was gone, Tyler was the only family she had left. Which was why he'd flown in a few days early, just to check out Marietta, and the people his grandmother had become so very attached to, namely Amanda Wright.

From Texas he'd done some research and what he'd learned about Amanda hadn't been all that reassuring, either. She was a credit risk. Not even the Bank of Marietta would give her a loan to close on the little house on Second and Church Streets. But Gram would, and did. His grandmother was generous to a fault and from what he was hearing in Texas, he feared she was being taken advantage of. He wouldn't be a very good grandson if he didn't come to Marietta and do some additional investigative work. Gram deserved to be protected, and she knew what his plans were for her. It wasn't as if he'd kept the Austin guesthouse a secret. He'd shared his plans with her from the beginning, and asked for her preferences in materials and layout. True, she hadn't been very enthused, but he believed with time she'd not just get used to the idea, but excited. He hoped to have her moved, if not by this spring, then by the end of summer so she wouldn't have to go through another harsh Montana winter on her own. It was just a matter of getting her to agree and then he'd handle all the moving arrangements.

And then he was there, at her little white house with the pale sage-green door. Her flowerboxes tucked beneath the tall windows flanking the front door were like little dollhouse flowerbeds with miniature conifers, ivy, and the fragrant paper-white. Lace curtains hung on the inside of the tall windows, concealing the interior. Little here seemed to change. Gram kept everything absolutely meticulous. He felt a tug of emotion as he knocked on the front door, thinking Gram had sometimes been the only constant in a world of change.

His parents struggled after Coby died, unable to grieve together, they'd grown apart, his dad always away, immersed in his work and his love of dangerous sports—skiing, mountain climbing, mountain biking—while his mother earned her real estate license and became one of the top Realtors in Los Gatos. Tyler hadn't known how to grieve, either. He'd been the younger brother his whole life and now the big brother he'd looked up to, the brother who'd never made a misstep, the brother who'd made his parents so very proud, was gone.

Tyler couldn't possibly fill Coby's shoes, and so he hadn't even tried. Instead he lost himself in his games, preferring the worlds he created over the real world filled with loss and pain.

Thank God for Gram. She might have lived halfway across the country but she was his rock, and his inspiration. She lived life with joy.

He knocked a second time, more firmly.

A lace panel lifted at one of the tall windows, and then moments later the front door flew. "Tyler!" His grandmother reached for him, patting his chest. "Look at you! What a surprise! I wasn't expecting you until Friday!"

He grinned. "Hello, Gram." He leaned over and gave her a firm hug and kiss on her soft, warm cheek. She was a little more slender, a little smaller, but still his beloved grandmother. "I arrived early."

"My goodness. Isn't this wonderful! Come in, come in. Are you hungry? Have you had lunch?"

"I just ate. I've checked into the Graff—"

"What? Why would you do that?"

"I've got some work to do while I'm here and until it's wrapped up, I'm better at a hotel with a business office."

His grandmother closed the front door and drew him down the hall and into her kitchen where she pulled out a chair for him to sit at her kitchen table. "How about coffee or tea then?"

"A cup of tea would be nice. It's cold out there."

"It's actually quite nice today for February, but it's that wind. It just chills one to the bone."

She filled the kettle and put it on a burner, before laying out two teacups and saucers, and filled a dainty blue-and-white-pattern plate with dainty sugar cookies she took from the freezer. "They're from Christmas when I did my baking," she said, as if reading his mind, "but they're still fresh. I treat myself to two a day, but that's all. I don't want to put weight on at my age because I'll never get it off."

He smiled affectionately as he settled back in his chair. She was wearing dark trousers paired with a gray sweater and another layered sweater piece. "You look fantastic, Gram. Very stylish."

She blushed and put a hand up to her chic silver pixie. "I just had my hair done today. Mandy gave it a little extra pizazz because she knew you were coming."

"Mandy? That's your hairdresser."

"Amanda Wright, yes. I've told you all about her."

"You have."

The kettle boiled and she filled her china teapot with hot water, and then added in the tea bags, placing all on a tray. When she moved to lift the tray, he rose. "Let me carry that, Gram."

"I can do it."

"I know, but I'm here, so let me help."

"You fuss over me too much."

"Maybe because Dad and Grandpa didn't fuss enough."

She gave him a quick, sharp look before following him to the table. "They did their best—"

"They didn't. They always put themselves first." And it crossed his mind the moment the words were out that he'd done the very thing for much of his life, too.

They'd all leaned on her, and taken advantage of her love, but had any of them ever considered what she needed? The realization strengthened his resolve to do better, and be there for her in the future. He'd accomplished so much in his career, but what was the point of success if he didn't have time for the people that mattered? And Gram mattered.

He held her chair, waiting for her to be seated before he sat down.

She gazed across the table, her blue eyes bright in her lined face, and yet the creases and wrinkles did nothing to diminish her beauty.

"It's really good to see you, Gram. It's been too long. I'm sorry I didn't make it at Christmas as planned."

"Your work keeps you busy."

"That's why I want you to join me—"

"How did you get away from work? You're here days early. I thought it was difficult taking time off?"

"It's a long way to come for just the weekend so this way I can work and see you. The best of both worlds."

She didn't immediately answer, focusing instead on arranging their cups and saucers and shifting the sugar bowl so it sat on the table halfway between them. After a minute she lifted the lid on the teapot and checked the tea before replacing it. "Just another minute to let it steep," she said.

"I'm in no hurry. I have nowhere to go."

Her blue gaze lifted and looked straight at him. "You look tired, Tyler. Is everything alright?"

"Just up early this morning for my flight." He patted his cheekbone. "Maybe I need some under eye cream... would that help with the puffiness? Or what would you suggest since you've cornered the market on beauty?"

She blushed, and laughed, just as he'd intended. "Thank you, but you can't distract me. I am concerned about you. You don't seem to have much of a life, Tyler. Are you dating? Have a girl... is there a significant other?"

"No."

"Why not?"

"It's hard balancing everything right now, Gram, but I'm working on it."

"Hmph."

"I am, really. And that's why I'm here. I want to make you a priority. I still feel bad about cancelling at the last minute my visit at Christmas."

"Tyler, I was married to a military man. I understand work and commitments, I do."

He watched her lift the teapot and begin filling their cups. "Speaking of commitments," he said carefully, "you mentioned to me on the phone that you've been meeting with your attorney. You're amending your will?"

"I haven't yet, no, but thinking about it." She set the pot down. "I've lived here for my entire life and want to leave something behind, something that can be my legacy."

He felt a painful knot in his chest. The idea of a world without his grandmother wasn't something he could contemplate.

"You are, of course, my legacy, too," she added, "but this town has meant a great deal to me and I'd like to do something for it... give something back to help those here who are less fortunate than me."

"I think that's an excellent idea. Are you thinking of starting a foundation, or is there a charity you're involved with?"

"There are a couple charities I give to, but what I want to do is less formal. I've someone I'd like to support."

"Someone?" he asked, trying to keep his voice neutral.

But she must have heard his tension because her head lifted and she gave him one of her no-nonsense looks. "I'm telling you so you'd be aware of my plans, not so you can judge."

"I'm not judging."

"Good. Because my personal finances are my own business." She gave him a sweet smile as if to soften her firm words. "I would hope at my age I don't have to explain my decisions to anyone."

He struggled to find the right words and the right tone as this was sensitive ground. "I just don't want you being taken advantage of, Gram."

"And who would be taking advantage of me, Tyler?"

"Any number of unscrupulous people—"

She added a small teaspoon of sugar to her tea and gave it a gentle stir. "Fortunately, I don't know anyone like that."

He hesitated, counting to ten, aware he was on perilous ground, but this was why he'd come here, and this was why he'd left Austin even though everything was chaotic.

He couldn't back away now. "Or friendly, well-meaning acquaintances, who might somehow make you feel responsible for their dreams or goals?"

"I don't know anyone like that, either."

"Gram, you are too kind for your own good."

She set her spoon down with a clink. "Tyler, what is this all about?"

Should he tell her? Should he not? Honesty won in the end. "The hair salon. Amanda Wright."

His grandmother didn't even blink. She just looked at him with her wide blue gaze, her expression impossibly trusting, and, for a moment, he thought he'd give anything for her serenity. But he'd never be her, and he could only do what he believed was right.

"Gram," he growled. "Stop being so difficult. *Talk* to me. Tell me what's going on."

"Nothing is going on."

"You've given Amanda Wright a small fortune."

"That is absolutely not true. I invested in her business. There is a big difference."

He took a sip of tea, and then another. Women were maddening. His grandmother the most maddening of all.

"Why would you do that?" he asked when he was certain his voice was pleasant.

"Because I believe in her. She's a smart young woman and this town needs her. She's good for Marietta, and I'm lucky to be her business partner."

He nearly choked on his tea. "Her business *partner?*"

"She has great ideas and I want her to make them happen."

It was so much worse than he thought. Amanda had never mentioned that his grandmother was her business partner either. There was no reason for him to have felt guilty investigating her. His only regret was that he hadn't checked her out more thoroughly. "Gram, your guesthouse is completely ready. It's all brand-new, and it's gorgeous. You'd love it. Please come live with me in Austin—"

"Austin?"

"Yes, Austin. It's where I live."

"I thought you were in San Jose. Isn't that where Silicon Valley is?"

"I moved to Texas two years ago, Gram. That's why I've been sending you books and magazines about Texas, and why I gave you that subscription to *Austin Monthly* for

Christmas, so you'd get to know the city and surrounding area—"

"You're the one that sent me the magazine? I thought it was one of those credit card companies."

"Why would they do that?"

"Because you get points with some cards, and if you don't use them, they give you a choice of magazines."

Tyler's brow furrowed. He honestly didn't know what to make of this conversation. Had he stayed away too long? Been too immersed in his work? Dear God, his grandmother wasn't going senile, was she?

She reached over and patted his arm. "Don't look so anxious. I just thought you were still in California." She gave him a quizzical glance. "Your mom is still there, isn't she? Because I could have sworn I got a Christmas card from her with a Los Gatos address."

"She's still in Los Gatos."

"So why did you move?"

"I sold my company to a Texas corporation and they wanted me to stay on as the head of Justice Games."

"Have you asked your mom to move?"

"No, because she's remarried, and you know that. I'm sure you got the same Christmas card of them in Florence that I did." And just saying the words felt like touching a bruise.

He was glad his mother was finally happy, just sorry it had taken her so long to find contentment. And yet they still never discussed Coby, and it had been more than fourteen years since his brother had died.

"She looks happy."

"She is," he said huskily.

Gram must have understood because she suddenly reached over and took his hand. "It's a good thing," she said firmly. "Your mother lost her oldest son, and then your father, and I'm glad she's found someone who can love her and give her life meaning."

Your mother lost her oldest son…

Coby.

He held her cool, dry fingers, her skin so soft in his. "Do you ever think about Coby?"

"Every day. I say a prayer for all my beautiful boys every day. Your grandfather, your father, and Coby. And then I say a prayer for you, thanking God I have you. And now you're here. What fun. Aren't I the luckiest?"

He, who didn't cry, or feel, felt as if she'd mashed his heart. "Oh, Gram, I hate that you're alone."

"Only I'm not. I'm not lonely, either. My life is wonderful and full. I'm blessed, truly." She released his hand and reached for the teapot and topped off their cups. "And I'm going to introduce you to my friends, starting with Amanda, tonight."

CHAPTER THREE

EVEN ON VIBRATE, Mandy's phone wouldn't stop buzzing and dancing around on the wooden shelf of her station. She knew who kept calling, too. She'd checked the phone the first three times. Bette clearly had something up her sleeve.

Finally on a break, Mandy listened to the voice messages accumulating.

Mandy, my grandson arrived early! He surprised me this afternoon. Please join us for dinner. Call me back, sweetheart, and let me know.

Mandy, can you join us for dinner? I'm thinking six o'clock. Where should we go for Tyler's first night here?

Mandy, I was going to make a reservation but wanted to be sure you could join us first...

Biting back a sigh, Amanda returned Bette's call. "Sorry, Bette, I've had back-to-back appointments. It turned out to be a very busy day."

"Does that mean you're too tired to join Tyler and me for dinner? I hope not. Would it help if I promised that it wouldn't be a late night?"

"Don't you want to have a night where you two can just

catch up?"

"Oh, we've had all afternoon, and we've made lovely plans for the week, but I want him to meet my friends, and I've told him all about you—"

"Oh, I wish you hadn't," Mandy said under her breath.

"Why not?"

"Because he won't understand why we're friends. He'll think I'm too young, or a bad influence, or something."

"He's my grandson, not my father."

Mandy laughed softly. She'd always enjoyed Bette's feisty sense of humor. "Just don't have too high of expectations, Bette. He might not like me."

"How can you say that? He'll take one look at you and fall in love—"

"I can assure you that is not going to happen."

"You never know."

"No, I do know. And you promised you weren't going to be doing any matchmaking."

"I'm not, Amanda, but I do think you two will hit it off. At least, I hope so, because I need your help. I need you to help him understand why Marietta is so special, and why you love Marietta just as much as I do."

"Oh, Bette."

"Just a couple days this week? Obviously not when you're working, but maybe one evening after work, and maybe Saturday or Sunday?"

"I work Saturdays."

"Then Sunday?"

"I'm not sure what I've planned," Amanda said, reluctant to commit to anything with regard to Tyler.

"But we're on for dinner tonight?"

Amanda sighed, knowing she'd already lost. She'd never been able to say no to Bette. "What time?"

"We'll pick you up at six."

"Just tell me where we're going and I'll meet you."

"But I don't know that yet. We'll just pick you up. Six o'clock?"

Mandy closed her eyes, counted to three, and then exhaled. "Sure."

HIS GRANDMOTHER GAVE him precise directions on how to get from her house on north Bramble, to the Wright Salon on the corner of Church and Second.

Tyler didn't have the heart to tell her he knew exactly where the salon was, because he'd been there earlier. And so, instead, he followed his grandmother's instructions, and pulled up in front of the salon, thinking perhaps Mandy was only now getting off work, but when she emerged from the house, she didn't come through the front door, but a side walkway, and she was wearing a black wool coat that reached her calves, black gloves, and black heels.

"Where are we going for dinner again?" he asked his grandmother as Amanda made her way toward the car.

JANE PORTER

"Rocco's. I love their ravioli."

"Is it a formal place?"

"No." And then she smiled as she caught sight of Amanda. "Oh, doesn't she look lovely? Mandy is always so stylish."

Tyler suppressed a sigh and climbed out of the car, not sure whether he was wildly underdressed or Amanda was wildly overdressed. All he knew for certain was that the prospect of having dinner with Amanda and his grandmother was making him nervous, and nothing made him nervous. At the office, he had a reputation for having nerves of steel.

Amanda approached him, her smile slightly mocking. "Hello."

He closed the distance between them, and extended a hand. "Ty Justice."

She arched a beautifully winged brow. "Ty, is it? Not Tyler?"

"My family calls me Tyler. My friends call me Ty."

"Amanda Wright," she answered, putting her gloved hand in his. "Only my family and close friends calls me Mandy."

It was a not so subtle reminder that he was not a friend.

His fingers closed around hers, his grip firm, firm enough to make her look up into his face. "It's nice to meet you, Amanda," he said gravely. "I've heard a great deal about you from my grandmother."

"I tried hard to get out of this dinner," she said quietly.

"I know. I was there when she was speaking to you. She's

very attached to you."

"Which you don't approve of." When he didn't immediately respond she shook her head. "Let's just get through the evening."

"Agreed."

Rocco's was just another block south on Church, the Italian restaurant tucked into the ground floor of an old brick building next door to the church.

Inside Rocco's, Amanda removed her black wool coat, revealing a peach plaid dress with black cap sleeves and a narrow black belt cinched around her waist. The bodice of the dress was fitted with tiny peach buttons from the waist to the neat Mandarin style collar, while the skirt was full, hitting just below her knee.

It might be thirty degrees outside, and late February, but Amanda looked like a breath of spring.

Her long golden blonde hair was down, curling over her shoulders like a 1940s actress, while small black button earrings matched the cap sleeves on her dress.

"Is that a vintage dress?" he asked her as they were seated at the big corner booth. Purple plastic grapes hung in generous clusters from the arbor ceiling, while murals of Tuscany covered the pale yellow walls. "Or new, to appear vintage?"

"It's a new dress, my sister's design. Charity and I make a lot of our clothes," she answered as she settled into the booth, next to Bette.

Bette reached over to pat Amanda's hand. "Mandy and Charity are extremely talented seamstresses. If Mandy wasn't such a good hair stylist, I'd tell her to open her own dress-making shop."

Tyler looked at Amanda and she shrugged. "Our family didn't have a lot of money. We did all of our shopping at second-hand stores. Knowing how to reinvent thrift store clothes saved face, and stretched a miniscule budget."

"And knowing how to cleverly adapt the house, turning it into your salon and home is another example of your money smarts," Bette said.

"You live in the back of the salon?" he asked her.

"Above," she corrected. "The upstairs is my lair." Her generous mouth curved, a dimple fluttering in her cheek, the dimple a tease.

His chest tightened. His body hardened. How could he desire someone he wasn't sure he even liked?

No, that wasn't fair. He liked her. But he wasn't sure he should like her.

That was the problem.

"How many rooms are upstairs?" he asked, trying not to focus on Mandy's soft lips, or the way her golden hair brushed her cheek making her look like a siren from a 1940s film.

"There were three tiny bedrooms and a bathroom, but I took down the wall between the two smaller bedrooms, turned it into a living room with a mini kitchen. It's on the cozy side, but perfect for my needs," she answered.

"You should see it," Bette enthused. "It's just delightful. Vintage and yet chic and modern. I'm so proud of everything she's achieved."

Tyler didn't miss how Amanda reached over and gave Gram's arm a little squeeze. "Thanks, Bette, but I had a lot of help with the house. You helped me—"

"Not much."

"No, you did, and then Charity helped me make the slip covers and drapes, and Sadie supplied all the furniture, and helped me pull it together."

"Sadie is a genius," Gram said nodding.

"Have you met her, yet?" Mandy asked him, her wide blue eyes locking with his.

His grandmother had blue eyes, light blue like water, but Amanda's reminded him of the Texas bluebonnet, intensely blue, and utterly captivating.

"She has a shop on Main Street," Amanda continued, as if her information was exactly the sort of thing he'd want to know. "The Montana Rose. She calls herself a shabby chic shop, but it's so much more than that. She has an amazing design aesthetic."

"And a new husband," Gram added. "She married Rory Douglas and it was supposed to be a small wedding but everyone in Marietta came. People were so happy for them." Her eyes suddenly watered. "I was so happy for them." She sniffled and reached for her napkin to dab her eyes, drying the moisture.

Tyler looked from Amanda to his grandmother and back again, feeling not just like an outsider, but a cynic. His grandmother was sentimental, yes, but to cry about a wedding?

"And why did everyone turn out for this particular wedding?" he asked, trying to indulge his grandmother even while fighting to hide his irritation. What kind of town was Marietta that everyone was excited about a wedding?

"Well, Rory is a Douglas."

"The acting family? Kirk, Michael, etcetera?" he replied.

"*No.* The Douglases of Paradise Valley. A local ranching family."

"I'm sorry, they don't mean anything to me," he answered.

His grandmother's jaw firmed. "Well, your father knew them. He went to school with Rory's father, and played sports, although to be fair, your father was a much better athlete—"

"Gram, I don't know them."

"They had a tragedy at their ranch. It's why the community cares so much about Rory, Quinn, and McKenna. Marietta loves and protects its own."

"Well, Bette, to be fair, the town loves and protects *some* of its own."

Tyler heard the mocking note in Mandy's voice and he turned his attention to her, focusing on the set of her jaw and the press of her lips. She suddenly didn't look as vivid and luminous as she had a few minutes ago. "Not everyone is equally embraced here?"

There was a flicker in her expression, a tiny tightening at her eyes, but before she could speak, his grandmother did. "Mandy has worked very hard for her success. I couldn't be prouder of her."

"Enough about me," Amanda answered, her faintly ironic smile returning. "Let's think about dinner. I hope you're both hungry, because I'm starving!"

TWO HOURS LATER, dinner was over and Amanda was climbing the stars to her upstairs apartment, wondering how someone as small and nonintimidating as Bette could have strong-armed Amanda into agreeing to take Tyler out with her friends for drinks after work tomorrow, even though Amanda's friends didn't do drinks on Wednesdays.

When Amanda had tried to say something of that nature, Bette dismissed her with a wave. "You do get together, don't you?"

"We do different things. Play pool or Yahtzee or cards—"

"Tyler likes all of those things. He's a bit of a card shark, too," his grandmother answered, "not that he'll admit it."

Amanda glanced at Tyler, giving him the chance to object, but he just shrugged. "It'd be great to meet your friends."

And so Amanda was stuck, and as she unlocked her front door, she told herself she didn't hate him, but she certainly wasn't happy to spend another evening with him, particularly not so soon.

She didn't hate him, she thought, locking the door behind her and turning on the hall lights, because he wasn't crass or arrogant or obnoxious. He was just...well, *him.* Smart, successful, attractive.

He looked like a romance cover model, carried himself like a professional athlete, and apparently was one of the most successful game developers in America today. Most women would love him. They'd say he was the complete package, and an amazing catch, and Amanda might even have been one of them, but that would have been before she knew he was Bette's grandson.

And now that she knew who he was, she really wanted to avoid him, but Bette had other plans. But there were lots of people who would be better tour guides than her. Rory and Sadie. Troy and Taylor. Trey and McKenna. Even her sister Charity would be better because Charity worked in real estate now and loved doing the whole here-is-Marietta-isn't-it-wonderful song and dance. Amanda wasn't interested in selling Marietta, and she definitely wasn't interested in making more awkward, small talk with Tyler. She and Tyler could fake being cordial in front of Bette, but they would never be real friends.

In her room, Amanda changed into her pajamas, pulled

her hair into a ponytail and washed her face. After applying one for favorite night creams, she brushed her teeth, and went to the cozy little living room with the steeply vaulted ceiling to watch TV. She clicked through her list of recorded programs and selected a rom com she'd taped but hadn't seen yet and was just watching the opening scene when her sister Charity called.

"We have to cancel tomorrow night," Charity said, when she answered.

Amanda paused her movie. "What's tomorrow night?"

"Tricia's surprise birthday party! How could you forget?"

The Wright sisters had been friends with Tricia Colton since they were young as they'd all grown up on the same street, Chance Avenue, and four years ago Jenny Wright had married Tricia's older brother, making them all even closer. "It's been a busy week," Amanda answered on a yawn, "and a *really* long day. But forget about that, why do we have to cancel the party?"

"Tricia's being sent to a travel agent training session in Denver and can't get out of it since she's the only one that really knows the new software they're using in the office."

"Does she know about the party?"

"No. It's a surprise. I invited everyone, so I'll call everyone and cancel, but do you still want to meet up with me? I haven't seen you in ages and could use a night out. Besides, from what I'm hearing, you've lots to tell me."

"I do?"

"You were seen with a very handsome man three times today."

"I was?"

"Sources tell me you were together at your hair salon, midafternoon at the Graff, and then again for dinner at Rocco's."

"Then your *sources* probably told you that he also happens to be Bette's grandson."

"Does that mean he's not attractive?"

"No, he is, but remember those old Harlequins we read in high school, the ones we got from the thrift store that were from the 70s and 80s? Where the hero was darkly handsome but also insufferable? Well, that's him. Handsome and insufferable."

"Ooh, that sounds promising."

"Not promising, not at all."

"I think I have to meet him myself."

"Why don't you invite him to Grey's? Have a drink with him, play some pool, fall in love—"

"Will I?"

Amanda glared into her phone. "Maybe, but hopefully not, because then you'd be living in Texas with him and Bette."

"Well, why don't you fall in love and live in Texas with him and Bette?"

"Because I love Marietta and I have a business here, and a smart-mouthed sister here."

"Then don't tell me to fall in love with him. That just shows me how much *you* already like him."

"I don't."

"I'll see you tomorrow after work at Grey's. And bring hot stuff. I'm dying to meet this guy," she answered with a laugh before hanging up.

Amanda growled, then hung up, and then laughed because Charity knew her better than anyone and Charity suspected what Amanda wasn't willing to admit—Tyler Justice was handsome and fascinating and everything Amanda might have liked—*if* he wasn't Bette's scheming grandson. But he was, and that was that.

AMANDA WASN'T A gym girl. Charity loved her Pilates and yoga and barre classes, but Amanda ran. She'd been on the cross-country team in high school, and running had helped her cope with anxiety in college, and she'd continued to run three to four times a week because it cleared her head and gave her a chance to focus on her goals before a long day at the salon.

Early Wednesday morning she woke and dressed for a run, pulling her long hair into a tight ponytail before knotting her running shoes, and venturing out.

Very few cars were on the streets at six. The sun was just beginning to peek over the mountains, casting a golden glow on the horizon. Amanda ran down Church Avenue, crossed

Court, and cut through Crawford Park to run along the banks of the Marietta River. This was her favorite route, and she followed the river past the rodeo and fairgrounds, deserted except for the stacks of lumber beginning to arrive for the new grandstand.

Her breath clouded on the cold air. Her ponytail swung back and forth. She was running at a clipped pace, but she'd settled into her stride, and her feet thudded on the ground in an even rhythm. As she ran, the sun continued to rise over the mountains, turning the sky yellow and pink. She loved having Marietta to herself. It always calmed her, centered her, and made her appreciate all that she'd accomplished. Life was good. Very good—

"Morning."

She startled at the male voice, and nearly tripped over her feet as she turned to face the runner who'd approached.

Tyler.

"Where did you come from?" she asked, pulse racing, but not the good kind. He'd genuinely scared her. She hadn't thought there was anyone else out here on the running path.

"I've been behind you since the fairgrounds. I wasn't sure it was you until just a moment ago." He was wearing black running pants and a black hoodie. "How far are you going?"

"To River Bend Park and back."

"That's where I'm heading."

"How did you know about the park?"

He reached into his pocket and pulled out a little map.

"The front desk had some running suggestions for guests. They said the trail to the park should be good since there's been no snow in a couple weeks." He shoved the map back into his pocket. "Would you object to company?"

"I don't want to hold you up," she answered.

"You won't. You're fast."

"Well, feel free to pass me anytime you want," she answered, starting to run again.

He dropped in next to her. "I will."

Running wasn't the same with Tyler next to her. She couldn't relax, and struggled to settle in to a steady tempo. Instead she felt as if she had two left feet. Her breathing was ragged. Her muscles felt tight. Her good mood was inexplicably gone.

At the park she slowed to a walk, and then she used one of the benches to stretch her hamstrings.

Tyler was doing the same. She tried to ignore him though. It was nearly impossible. He wasn't breathing hard at all, and his running pants hugged his quads and hamstrings, while the fabric wrapped his glutes. He had long, muscular legs, and a great butt. She hated that she noticed, but he had big shoulders and muscles everywhere. From a purely physical perspective, he was pretty much perfect. But from a personal perspective, he was really getting under her skin.

"Go ahead," she said, gesturing to the path. "I think I'm going to just take it easy and walk back."

"Happy to walk back with you, unless you don't want the company?" He glanced at her, his green gaze inscrutable.

No, she didn't want company, but how could she tell him that? She promised Bette that she would be nice to him, and she would be nice to him, even if it killed her.

"Company would be lovely," she lied.

His lips quirked. He looked amused. "How often do you run?"

"I try to get out here a couple mornings a week, and then in summer, I'll run after work, because we have such lovely long days. In June and July it stays light until well after nine o'clock, but then we pay for it in winter with really short days."

"Do you have any other favorite places to run?"

"In good weather I'll head up to Miracle Lake, but I won't do it now. Too much ice still. And if I'm short on time, I'll do a big loop around downtown, from Crawford Park, around the courthouse, down Bramble, over to the Wolf Den, past the Depot, the Graff, to the park, and back home."

"The Wolf Den?"

"It's a bar, a bit on the seedy side." She flashed him a smile. "But there are plenty of men who like it. Karaoke on Mondays, ladies' mud wrestling on Thursdays and pole dancing nightly."

"Here in Marietta?"

"We're right off the highway. Truckers love it. You

should check it out."

"I don't think Gram would approve."

"I won't tell her."

"Ha! Somehow I doubt that. I think the two of you are in a league of your own."

"Maybe we are," she said with a wink, before taking off, sprinting down the path paralleling the river.

She heard him closing in behind her, so she kicked it into higher gear, and ran faster, harder, harder than she'd gone in a long time, running as if the finish line was just ahead and a first-place finish was at stake. She ran the last mile that way, arms and legs pumping, heart pounding, and it was electric. She felt fantastic, strong and free. Mandy only slowed when her path took her up to the courthouse in Crawford Park, the historic copper dome gleaming in the sunrise. Turning, hands on her hips, she glanced behind her, and there was Tyler, right on her tail.

He flashed her a grin. "Nice way to finish the run," he said. He wasn't breathing hard at all. His cheeks weren't even red with exertion.

"I thought I lost you."

"Not a chance. Was having too much fun."

She wasn't sure what he meant by that, so she let the comment ride. "I'm going to grab a coffee from Java Café before I head home. If you feel like tagging along, I'll point out places you might want to know about."

"Sounds good," he answered. "Especially the coffee part."

They crossed the park with Amanda pointing out landmarks. "Our courthouse, and then to the right is our library, built around the same time as the courthouse, in the 1880s. Most of Marietta was constructed during the big copper boom of the 1880s-1890s. The oldest building on Main Street is Grey's Saloon. I think that one dates from the late 1870s. Grey's has been written up in numerous Montana magazines as one of the oldest bars in the state that still pours liquor today."

She glanced at him as they crossed Court Street and started down Main, debating whether she should mention drinks and pool tonight at Grey's. Did she want him there? What would he think of the invite?

Still uncertain, she pointed out other businesses. "Main Street Diner is an institution in Marietta. It's been a diner since the 1920s or 30s. Before that it was a grocery store and mercantile. Great big breakfasts until eleven, and home-style cooking the rest of the day. I rarely go for dinner but Charity and I always head to the diner for pie after movie night. On the left is my friend Sadie's shabby chic business, Montana Rose. Her space was once part of the old antique mall, which was turned into our first Mexican restaurant. The restaurant just opened but I haven't been there yet, not sure why as I heard it has amazing carne asadas and hand-shaken margaritas."

"The only kind of margarita," he replied.

The tour continued as they crossed First Street. "Grey's

is on our right, and our Bank of Marietta is on the left. Best cowboy boots in town are here, at Marietta Western Wear and then the pharmacy on this corner—I'll tell you more about that later—and Java Café is just ahead, on our right, with world famous Copper Mountain Chocolates on the other side of Main, next to the florist."

"Is the chocolate shop famous?"

Amanda grinned and shook her head. "Not world famous, no, but here in Marietta, it's a big deal. I love the salted caramels. Charity loves the hot chocolate. And everyone loves Sage, the owner. You'll have to stop in and introduce yourself."

"Your salon isn't far from here."

"Nope. Just one street over." She smiled at him. "I spend a lot of time here at Java Café. Their coffee is so much better than mine and they have a great rewards program for customers. Every sixth coffee is free."

Once inside the Java Café they ordered their coffees and Tyler also ordered breakfast to go.

While they waited for his toasted egg bagel sandwich he asked her, "What do you think I should know about Marietta?"

"What did your dad tell you about Marietta?"

"Not much. He wasn't particularly fond of Marietta."

"Really? Why?"

"I don't know. He didn't talk about it much. I got the impression that it's quite conservative."

"It's not the most liberal town, no, but I've found it's also surprisingly open-minded."

"And it's small, so small that everyone knows everyone else's business."

"Well, there is some truth to that. We have our share of gossips, and when things get slow in winter—we have really long winters some years—people talk. It's not necessarily malicious… at least, most of it isn't. Carol Bingley and her friends are another matter."

"Carol Bingley?"

"She and her husband own the drugstore we just passed. She seems to know everything, about everyone, so my tip to you, is go to the new CVS pharmacy in the shopping center and skip Marietta Drug downtown if you don't want to become fodder for the rumor mill."

"Completely agree."

"Wow. That's a first. We actually agreed on something?"

"I think there's a lot we agree on." He ticked his points off on his fingers. "We both love my grandmother."

"True."

"It seems we both like to start our day with a morning run."

She was trying not to smile. "Okay."

"And apparently we both like a good margarita."

"You say that, but how do I know if that's true? I have no evidence."

He smiled at her, his smile warmed his green eyes and

made him altogether too appealing. "Do I need to prove myself?" he answered. "Take you to Rosita's for a tequila taste-off?"

She laughed. Yes. "No."

"It sounds as if I do. It sounds as if my masculinity has been called into question—" He broke off as she giggled, and his eyebrow lifted. "I'm determined to defend my honor. Rosita's tonight, six thirty?"

"I can't. I've plans. And I thought you were having dinner with your grandmother tonight?"

"We are, at five fifteen, for the early bird special."

"In that case, stop by Grey's tonight and I'll introduce you to Charity. We're meeting up around seven."

CHAPTER FOUR

TYLER WALKED BACK to the Graff, carrying his breakfast sandwich and coffee. He smiled at the doorman, and then held the elevator doors open for a mother with a big stroller and a tearful toddler who didn't want to exit the elevator.

As he headed up to his room, he whistled part of a tune and then smiled ruefully as he realized he was whistling. He had no idea why he was in such a good mood, because he was in a great mood this morning. He'd slept surprisingly well, and he'd had a good run, and he'd enjoyed the tour and banter with Amanda. So it was hard to say why he was feeling relaxed, and even happy. He rarely felt happy, not because he liked being unhappy, but simply because it was an emotion he didn't focus on.

He tended to focus on work. He hadn't had a date since before he moved to Texas. If he went out in Austin, he went with a group from the office. Work was consuming. It had always been consuming, not because there was any external pressure to succeed, but just because he loved what he did, and he found it hard to balance work and personal life, so his personal life became his professional life, and vice versa, allowing him to focus on work all the time.

In his world, there was always another game, another challenge, another opportunity, to the point that his sole identity was that of being Tyler Justice, of Justice Games. He didn't have a life outside of his company, and it'd been this way for years, and he didn't mind... or at least, he hadn't thought he minded until he got to Texas and realized there were huge holes in his life, holes where people and hobbies were supposed to be.

It was why he wanted Gram with him, and it was why he'd built the guesthouse in his backyard for her. He had a large property just south of Austin and her new house would give her a great deal of independence. She could entertain her friends, and come and go. She'd love his neighborhood, too. Best of all, she'd be safe, and he could keep an eye on her.

But now that he was in Marietta, he was beginning to understand why Gram loved it and how moving her to Austin wasn't exactly the slam dunk he'd thought it was. And then there was the fact that he'd lived in Austin two years, and if it didn't yet feel like home, how did he expect his eighty-year-old grandmother to settle in?

"SO IS HE coming?" Charity asked that evening as they nursed drinks in a corner booth at Grey's.

"He said he was," Amanda answered, flipping her long hair back over her shoulder, telling herself she wasn't eager or excited or interested in Tyler in any way, because he was unsuitable in every way. "He's coming after dinner with Bette. They were going for an early bird special somewhere."

"Who does an early bird special in Marietta?"

"I think the Chinese restaurant does, and then Flintworks was trying something... more of a happy hour kind of thing, but maybe Bette thought Tyler would like it."

"So what does he look like?"

"He's tall, at least six feet one, with a great bod."

"Brown hair, light eyes, great face?"

"Yes."

"Well, I think your Tyler Justice has arrived and is on his way to our table now."

Amanda glanced over her shoulder, and her pulse did a wicked jump as she spotted him. He was wearing a black button-down shirt beneath a dark jacket, faded denims, and work boots and looked more like a model in a fashion catalogue than an ordinary man.

"And he *is* really good-looking," Charity mumbled under her breath. "No wonder everyone's talking."

"It's the haircut. You should have seen him before he came to me," Amanda deadpanned.

Charity laughed and Amanda scooted over in the booth, making room for Tyler. "You made it," she said.

"I did." He dropped into the booth next to her, filling

the space she'd just created. The man was big, and his shoulders were so broad she felt the need to scoot further to put space between them. Fortunately, he didn't seem to notice.

"Gram wasn't sure why she wasn't invited, though," he added, removing his jacket.

His black shirt was only unbuttoned by a few buttons but the fabric was snug over his shoulders and fitted across the chest, emphasizing muscles and how physically fit he was. "We can go get her," Amanda answered a little breathlessly, pulse still not quite steady.

"No, she's ready for *Wheel of Fortune* and then bed. She's tired. Today was movie day."

"Did you go?"

"I did, and met eighteen of her closest friends." He looked across the table to Charity and smiled, showing his dazzling white teeth. "I'm Tyler," he said, extending his hand, introducing himself.

"Charity," she said, giving his hand a shake. "The middle Wright sister."

"The clothes designer sister," he said. "Amanda wore one of your dresses last night."

Charity blushed, but looked pleased. "I just sketch them. Mandy sews them."

"You did the cuffs and buttons," Mandy protested. "I still can't get my buttonholes perfect."

"That's because you get frustrated and give up." Charity

turned to Tyler. "Mandy has the temper in the family. You don't want to make her mad."

Amanda rolled her eyes. "I don't have a temper."

Charity grinned and shrugged. "Just saying, don't make her mad."

"Noted," he answered.

The waitress came around and they all ordered a beer and sat talking for the next hour, the conversation easy, particularly as Charity and Tyler hit it off, almost a little too well, Amanda thought, battling envy. It was just that Charity was normally the shy one in the family, but tonight she was positively gregarious, and glowing as if she was that famous Farrah Fawcett poster from the 70s, the one of Farrah wearing nothing but a red swimsuit, her thick tousled golden mane, and a perfect smile showing white perfect teeth.

Amanda silently scolded herself for being jealous. There was no reason to be insecure. It wasn't as if she had feelings for Tyler, nor was she invested in him in any way. Bette had asked her to be nice to him, and show him Marietta, and she had. She was. If Tyler and Charity wanted to flirt, that was their business, not hers.

But after an hour of listening to Tyler and Charity talk and laugh, Amanda felt ready to call it a night. If Charity was going to fall in love with Tyler, she didn't want to be here to watch it happen.

"I think I'm good," she said when the waitress came by to see if they'd like another round. "Tomorrow is my long day, and I should head home and get some sleep."

"I should head home, too," Charity said, stretching. "I'm reading a great book and I'm dying to find out what's going to happen next."

"Oh? What are you reading?" Tyler asked, handing the waitress his credit card to cover the bill.

"Please don't pay for us," Amanda said, fishing in her purse for cash. "Let's each take care of our own."

"Yes," Charity agreed, pulling out her wallet.

"I've got this one, one of you can buy next time," he answered, before looking at Charity. "So what book did you say you were reading?"

"*Taming His Fierce Forbidden Heart.*" Charity gave him an innocent look. "Have you read it?"

For a moment Tyler looked nonplussed, and then he smiled crookedly. "No, no I haven't."

"It's a romance," Amanda murmured dryly.

"I gathered," he answered.

"A very good romance, too," Charity added, eyes bright with silent laughter. "I can loan it to you when I'm finished. It's very romantic, and quite sensual."

"I do think that's my cue to leave," he said, rising from the booth.

"Mine, too," Amanda agreed, sliding out as well.

"Anyone need a ride?" he offered as the three of them walked toward the door.

"I have my car," Charity said, holding up her keys.

Amanda zipped up her down coat. "I'm on foot, but I like the walk."

"I'll walk you home then," Tyler offered.

"It's one block over, Ty. I've got this."

"I know, but my grandmother would never forgive me if she found out I let you walk home alone."

"That is a valid point," she conceded, smiling. As they started down the street she glanced at him. "What's Austin like? I hear it's a great city."

"I'm still getting to know it, but it has lots of great restaurants and music scene. Sadly, I haven't been out as much as I would have liked." He grimaced. "I have a tendency to spend all my time at work, but the office downtown is nice. Big building, lots of windows, very modern."

She shook her head. "A workaholic."

"I do work a lot, but I love it."

"So why did you sell your company to someone else?"

"I knew the only way for my company to reach the next level was to have more money, and I could take it public, or, I could sell it to a company already public. In the end, I decided that TexTron made the most sense."

"Is it everything you hoped it'd be?"

He hesitated. "Sometimes we have to make hard choices. I don't have the control I used to, but Justice Games can leverage its power and position in a way it couldn't before." He glanced at her. "I confess I have an ulterior motive for walking you home. There was something Gram said that I wanted to ask you about, if you don't mind."

The moon was full and bright in the sky, and their footsteps echoed on the pavement. "I don't mind," she answered. "What did you want to know?"

"Gram mentioned yesterday she was your business partner, and I was just wondering who you used as your attorney when you drew up your business papers."

She shot him a confused glance. "Excuse me?"

"Gram said she'd gone into business with you——"

"No, she didn't," Amanda said firmly. "Bette's not my business partner. It would have been fun if she had become my partner, because she's a great lady, and I enjoy her very much, and admire her even more, but she isn't my partner in any size, shape, or form."

"Why would she say she was your partner then?"

"Because she enjoys being around the salon, and likes being a part of things?"

He was silent as they crossed the street. "How much do you know about her finances?" he asked as they approached Church Street.

"Only what she's chosen to tell me."

"Which is…"

"That your grandfather left her comfortably well-off."

"She didn't show you any numbers, bank statements, savings statements, nothing like that?"

"No, nor would I want to see her financials. It's none of my business."

"But you're aware that my grandmother is wealthy."

"I see where this is going, and I don't like it." Amanda stopped in front of her gate, arms folding over her chest, indignation warring with hurt. "I have not befriended your grandmother for financial gain. She has been my client from the very beginning, which is nearing nine years now. I care for her, and enjoy her company immensely, and I would never exploit her friendship in any way. Good night."

CHAPTER FIVE

Amanda had gone to bed outraged, and had woken up still upset, and hurt. It really bothered her that Tyler would think she'd take advantage of Bette in any way. They'd spent time together. Had dined together. Run together. Laughed together.

How could he still think so poorly of her?

Normally she didn't run on Thursdays, but today she ran, going north on Collier, past the elementary school and junior high, passing the community park until she reached the high school track, where she'd run the stairs in the small stadium. She hadn't run stairs in months but it was exactly what she needed today. Up and down, up and down she went, until her heart was pounding and her quads burned and she'd burned out the negative emotions.

Amanda wasn't just calm, when she returned home, she was feeling cheerful, even buoyant, and after coffee and scrambled eggs, was ready for whatever the day would bring.

Or thought she was ready, until she saw Tyler Justice headed up the front walk to the salon's front porch.

All cheer and goodwill disappeared as she watched him

through the front window, open the door, and step inside the salon. Even in a heavy coat, navy plaid shirt, boots and chinos, he looked casually elegant, and ridiculously confident.

On someone else it'd look like a plaid shirt and chinos and work boots, but Tyler's coat fit his broad shoulders and the plaid shirt somehow accented his muscular torso and lean waist instead of hiding it. His chinos weren't too baggy and they wrapped his thighs, highlighting the muscle there.

And then he had that face, and he did have great hair…

She heard voices in the entry. He was here. In her space.

She didn't have time—or energy—for this. What could he possibly want from her now? After last night she had no desire to see him ever again.

She prayed Emily was sending him away, telling him how busy Amanda's morning was, with a first appointment—

"Good morning," he said, entering the former living room, which was now the main styling room in the salon.

She didn't even try to smile. She wasn't in the mood. "What can I do for you?"

"I'm your nine am appointment."

"You are not."

"I am." He reached up, touched the back of his hair. "I thought I could maybe get a little more off. It's a bit longer than I'm used to. But I'm paying for it—"

"You don't have to pay for me to fix a cut—"

"I did like it. It was Gram who thought it was a little long."

"I don't charge customers to fix a mistake—"

"It wasn't a mistake. You gave me a great cut. I just think I'd like a different one now."

Amanda closed her eyes, shook her head, thinking she couldn't do this with him. "I'll give you to a different stylist."

"I don't want a different stylist."

She opened her eyes, looked up at him, gaze meeting, locking with his. "You don't want me, either."

"If I misjudged you—"

"You misjudged me."

"I'm sorry."

He sounded sincere and Amanda swallowed around the lump in her throat. She appreciated the apology, she did, but it didn't change the fact he'd thought the worst of her. He'd believed she'd been taking advantage of Bette. It wasn't even a question in his mind. He really thought she was that unprincipled...

It hurt. A lot.

Having grown up with very little, having been lumped in with "the poor Wright sisters" her entire life, she was sensitive to speculation and slights. One of the reasons she'd always avoided dating wealthy men was that after the whole fiasco between her sister Jenny and her former fiancé, Charles, Amanda didn't want anyone to think she was a social climber, or trying to marry up, or marry for money. She didn't want money. She wanted self-respect.

The entire reason she and her sisters worked so hard was to prove to the world—as well as themselves—that they weren't welfare girls, or poor white trash. Just because they'd been raised on thrift store clothes and handouts, didn't mean they'd remain in poverty, dependent on others.

They didn't need to be taken care of, and they were good people, smart, loving, valuable. And yet somehow just a few careless words on Tyler's part had wounded her, getting under her skin, making her feel less than.

It wasn't right. Not just what he thought of her, but that she allowed his opinion to upset her so much. She should be stronger. She should have more pride, and more resolve.

Amanda folded her arms over her chest. "I need to make a few things clear, just in case there is any confusion. Your grandmother didn't pay for this house. She doesn't own any of the salon. She gave me a loan, a loan that has already been paid back, in full, with interest."

"That's good."

"I paid her back with an interest rate *better* than she was getting from the bank."

"That's very good."

"Yes, it is." She hesitated. "But just to be sure you're fully in the know, she did give me another gift, it was over the holidays. It was something she owned."

"Tell me it wasn't her silver," he muttered.

Her gaze narrowed and met his, expression cool and disapproving.

"That was a joke," he said, lifting his hands.

"Many a joke was said in jest," she retorted, crossing to the window to push the pale pink silk drape and gesture to the back of the property where a small RV sat parked in the driveway next to her detached garage. "It's her old motorhome. It's going to be my mobile salon one day, so that I can go visit my clients when they can't come to me." Amanda dropped the curtain and turned to him. "It hasn't been refurbished yet. I don't have the means to redo it, but your grandmother is excited by the idea that I could provide mobile beauty services to seniors in Crawford County, particularly the seniors who are housebound. She wants to help me fix it up, but I've refused all offers. I don't want her money, but renovating the RV is part of my plan for later this year, and if I can't do it this year, then next year for sure. But women should feel beautiful no matter their income, or their age, and I appreciate your grandmother's faith in me." What she didn't add, was that Bette was the first person, outside of her sisters, who'd ever truly believed in her and Bette's faith in her had been exactly what Amanda had needed as a young woman uncertain if she could be the person she wanted to be.

"I think it's a great idea."

"You do?"

"I do."

She searched his face, looking to see if he was being straight with her, and she didn't see anything in his expression that made her uneasy or suspicious. "So you really want a haircut?"

"I really do."

"And you trust me not to just shave your head, or do something horrendous?"

One dark brow lifted quizzically. "I would think you'd hate to destroy your perfect review status."

"I do like my five-star reviews."

"Then I don't think you'd honestly shave my head, or nick it, or anything else diabolical you might be imagining."

She pointed to her chair. "Have a seat."

"Aren't we going to go to the shampoo area?"

"Yes. After I put your cape on."

"I do like a good cape."

It was all she could do to keep from smiling. Perhaps her lips did twitch a little. But she didn't want to be amused, or entertained. He was awful as men went. Arrogant and egotistical, as well as dictatorial. Again she flashed to her old Harlequins and beloved Barbara Cartlands. "You're used to getting your way," she said, stepping behind her dark pink chair.

"In my world, things generally go my way," he admitted, sitting down.

She gave the folded cape a hard flick of her wrist, making the material crackle before she settled it around his big shoulders. As she fastened the snap closed, her fingers brushed the back of his neck and she felt a sharp frisson of sensation crackle through her. Amanda exhaled hard, suddenly breathless, suddenly feeling far too aware of him, not as a client, but as a man. She really didn't want to spend the next twenty to thirty minutes touching him. "I'll have one of the girls shampoo you," she said huskily, "and then bring you back to my chair."

His eyes met hers in the mirror. "If you don't think I need my hair washed—"

"It's easier to give a good cut when it's clean. I have one of my interns here today, and I need to use her, and I thought you'd probably appreciate her shampooing you instead of doing the cut?"

The expression in his eyes seemed to doubt every word she was saying. "Good call," he answered, and then as his gaze met hers in the mirror, and held for what was far too long, she felt her pulse do a crazy, dramatic spike, and thump away.

He was so not what she needed, or wanted—well, needed.

For some reason she seemed to want him, but she didn't want to think about that now, not with him back in her chair for the next twenty to thirty minutes.

She turned away, tucking a long blonde tendril behind her ear, something she did when nervous, and then plucked it back out because it didn't belong behind her ear, but down, framing her face, matching the piece on the other side. "Shelley," she called, waving her nineteen-year-old intern forward. "Give him a good shampoo and then bring Mr. Justice back. Also, find out if he'd like a coffee, tea, or water—"

"Water would be great," he answered her, rising from the chair. "Thank you, Amanda."

The husky note in his deep voice contradicted the gleam in his eye and her face grew hot. "I'll have your water here for you when you return, Tyler." Then she stalked to the kitchen, grateful for five minutes to herself, needing the time to pull herself together.

He was just a customer.

She was going to give him a cut.

That was all.

There was no need for nerves or drama. Nothing was happening. No need to feel so terribly unsettled.

She filled a glass of water for him from their water dispenser and returned to her station, placed the glass on the counter for him before laying out her scissors and combs on the pale pink towel on her silver rolling tray.

"You like pink," he said, when he appeared a minute later and sat back down in the dark pink chair.

"I do. As you can see it's my signature color for the salon."

"And yet you only wear red lipstick."

He'd noticed? She didn't know why that made her feel

all fluttery on the inside. "I don't wear pink. I don't think I own anything pink."

"So why make it your salon's signature color?"

"It's fresh and pretty. Feminine."

"I'd think it'd discourage your male clientele."

"It hasn't so far. And honestly, if I they're not comfortable with my salon they can go somewhere else. There are plenty of other salons and barbershops in Marietta. The last thing I want a man feeling is insecure with his masculinity."

"I'm not insecure," he said. "I'm just curious why you'd risk fifty percent of your potential customer base? It doesn't sound like good business."

"My established client base would come to me even if my salon was painted bright pink—"

"Come on."

"It's true. They're coming to see me, and they're secure enough in themselves to not mind a feminine environment. Now hold still, because I have very sharp scissors and you have a very exposed neck."

He was silent for the next twenty minutes, something she was grateful for so she could concentrate on taking off more length without making him look like a shorn sheep. It wasn't hard, actually, because he had great bone structure and with his broad brow and strong jaw, he could wear his hair virtually anyway and be appealing—

"Why not try to market to men?" he asked, interrupting her thoughts.

She put the scissors down, ran her fingers through the sides of his hair, and then the top, checking to be sure it was all even. "Because the world already caters to men. Everything is about making men secure and comfortable. Just look at Main Street here in Marietta, for example. All those solid brick buildings, all those wooden storefronts...they're not feminine. This town isn't feminine. It's a solid, practical town and I wanted to create something pretty and inviting for women, so I did."

"I'm just saying you could have put green chairs in here instead of pink and then men would have felt equally welcome."

She paused, gaze locking with his in the mirror. "You're saying you don't feel welcome because my chairs are pink?"

"The towels are pink. The front door is pink. Your apron is pink."

"And your cape is black. I could have made that pink as well, I suppose."

"Or green. Green is a great neutral color, gender friendly—"

"Gender friendly, that's interesting." Amanda reached for the jar of hair pomade on her shelf and rubbed some of the crème between her hands, warming it, thinning it, before dragging her fingers through his hair, giving the front a lift, spiking a little for height, and then smoothing the shorter sides. "I was going to give the salon a fresh coat of paint this spring. Maybe I should do it pink. Pink siding with white trim."

He rolled his eyes. "Your front door is already pink."

"So I'll paint the door white. Or maybe a soft aqua blue."

"You wouldn't really paint your salon pink."

"Why not?"

"It'd kill your business—"

"It wouldn't."

"It'd be a huge waste of money."

"Not if I did it myself."

"You wouldn't."

She felt her lips curve, the corners tilting up, hiding her pride and determination because Amanda Wright never backed down from a challenge. "You clearly don't know me."

YOU CLEARLY DON'T know me.

Amanda's words stayed with him all morning, nagging at his conscience. On one hand, she was right—he didn't really know her, but he wondered about the financial difficulties she'd had, and her damaged credit.

Unfortunately he couldn't stay in Marietta as planned. TexTron was in discussion with another tech giant, and if there was going to be a merger or acquisition, he wanted to be there at the office in Austin.

He picked up sandwiches and salads from Java Café and had lunch with his grandmother at her kitchen table.

"This is fun," she said happily, as they plated their meal on her pretty floral china.

"It's a picnic at home."

He smiled at her enthusiasm. She was so incredibly good-natured. He'd never met anyone so determined to live life to the fullest and she was so happy he was here in Marietta now. It wasn't easy to disappoint her, and she would be disappointed when he broke the news that he needed to return to Texas early.

"I've heard some rumors about work that are making me uneasy, Gram," he said as they finished their meal and he cleared their lunch dishes. "I need to get back to Austin and I should return sooner than later."

"What is happening?"

"I'm not totally sure. That's the issue."

"Then of course you would want to be there." Gram folded her hands in her lap. "When will you return?"

He put the plates in the sink, and ran the water for a moment. "Today." He turned off the water and faced her. "I'm on a six o'clock to Denver."

"Today?"

"I'll be back soon."

"From you, that could mean months."

"No, I promise. Soon. A couple weeks at the most."

Her expression crumpled. "I was just getting used to having you here."

He returned to the table and sat down close to her chair.

"Gram, why don't you come with me? Your house is ready—"

"You mean, fly with you tonight?"

"Yes. There are available seats on the flight. I already checked. Pack a bag and come with me. Make it a trial run, see what you think. I have a feeling you'll love it."

"And what about Marietta? And my bridge group? We're playing on Friday. And then there's a birthday luncheon for Barbara on Saturday. Do I just be a no-show for that?"

"Don't you want to have an adventure? See something new?"

"Every day is an adventure here. You never know if it's going to rain or sleet or snow."

"I hate leaving you, Gram."

"You mean, you hate leaving me to all my fun?" She patted his hand. "Don't fret. I'll pace myself."

"I'm serious."

"And so am I. All you do is work. While I get to see friends and contribute to the well-being of my younger friends."

"Amanda."

"Yes, Amanda. I love seeing what she's doing… building her business, expanding into a mobile salon as well as her ideas of a new senior center. Have I told you about that? It's truly marvelous—"

"Gram, I need you to be honest. Has she asked you for financial support?"

"Never. Not once."

"Do you ever feel guilty that she's struggling—"

"No, and she's not struggling anymore. She did for a bit, and I think it's because the other salon she managed wasn't pleased she was leaving to open her place, and made it difficult for her to take her clients, but ultimately, it all sorted out."

She kept on talking, telling him things he already knew, how the pink station chair was always open and available for her at the Wright Salon, and how at any time she wanted an appointment, her chair was waiting and Amanda would make herself available. But at the same time, she never took advantage of the open chair policy, although she did like to drop in and sit down and watch Amanda work, or chat when Mandy had a moment.

"We've formed a lasting bond," she added, "and it's not a recent thing. We've become good friends over the years."

"What do you talk about?" he asked, torn between exasperation and curiosity.

"Everything. Marietta happenings, like the upcoming St. Patrick's Day Ball at the Graff, to the grandstand construction just starting at the Rodeo Fairgrounds, to new romances blossoming in town." She blushed. "I'm a bit of a matchmaker here in town. Two relationships and counting."

"You do know that real friends don't have to give each other expensive gifts."

"Gifts? What gifts?"

"The RV. I saw it parked in her driveway behind her salon. It was yours, wasn't it?"

"It's hers now."

"Why?"

"She needs it, I don't."

"You can't just give away everything you have."

Bette's chin rose, temper sparked. "Did you want the old RV? Is that the issue?"

"No."

"Then what is your problem?"

"The loan... the RV... I just... worry."

"Do you know why I gave her the RV?" his grandmother asked, and when he didn't answer she filled the silence. "Mandy was one of the few people who came to see me at the hospital when I was recovering from my surgery. And she didn't just come with some flowers or chocolates. No, she came to the hospital and did my hair. She washed it, and set it, and made me feel beautiful when I was at an all-time low—and then she came to the house every week, for the next eight weeks to do my hair. She came to me because I'd given up. I'd lost your grandfather a few years before, and then your dad died, and I had both my hips replaced and a part of me just stopped fighting. I felt tired and useless and for eight weeks Mandy came every Tuesday night with dinner, and we'd eat together and she'd do my hair, and then while my hair was drying we'd watch a show, and she wouldn't take a penny for any of it. She said we were friends, and that's what friends did for each other."

Gram gave him a quelling look. "And so, Tyler, I appreciate that you're a big city guy, and you make all this money and know a thing or two about people and motives, but you're wrong about her, *and* you're wrong to speak to me as if I'm senile and throwing my money around. But if I should want to throw my money around, well, that's fine, too, because it's my money, and I'm an adult, and I have the right to do what I want with my property and investments."

For a moment there was just silence. She was waiting for him to reply but for the life of him, he couldn't think of a thing to say.

"I'm just trying to look out for you, Gram," he said at length.

"But at what cost? You risk alienating everyone by being so mistrustful."

"Dad would want me to take care of you."

"You forget, I was *his* mother."

They were just going around in circles, he thought, and it was incredibly frustrating because his intentions were good. He wasn't trying to hurt anyone. He was trying to be a protective grandson. "I love you, Gram. That's all."

"And I love you, which is why maybe you need to step away from your computer and games and open your eyes to all the wonderful people and things in this world. Life is so much bigger than a video screen."

"I know that."

"I'm not so sure you do, because ever since Coby died,

you've made games your world, and I love that you're creative and ambitious. I admire how you turned a hobby into a career, but it seems to me you've left out the most important thing, which is people."

CHAPTER SIX

TYLER WAS RELIEVED to be back in Texas so he could be on-site for the discussion about TexTron's future, but Marietta was never far from his thoughts, even though his visit felt like it had been one complication after another, with the complication being Mandy, Mandy, Mandy.

He sat through an intense four-hour meeting listening to the board of directors mandate change—grateful he wasn't the CEO of TexTron, but merely the head of the corporation's game division, and scribbled notes to himself regarding his division's numbers and profitability. Justice Games was doing well, he knew that much, but he was less clear on the other arms of TexTron's entertainment division.

While making notes, he found himself thinking of Amanda again, namely the thing she'd said to him the first day they met, that people needed entertainment. They needed a way to escape the world's chaos... or unplug from the world... something along those lines.

She understood people. That was what made her successful. Not the pink palette, or her retro style, but her empathy, and her desire to make people—women—feel special, and valuable.

She was also beautiful and smart and incredibly frustrating. The fact that he was attracted to her just made everything more difficult. It had been years since he'd felt this way about a woman. And yet she'd caught his attention, and worse, gotten under his skin and he couldn't stop thinking about her. Even in the middle of tense meetings.

Why *her*? He didn't want to want her. He didn't want to feel this pull toward her. He hadn't needed two haircuts. But he couldn't stay away from her...

So Texas was definitely a better place for him until he figured out how to manage her, and the tug and pull that made him want to bring her close and hold her, and lightly stroke the sweep of her cheekbones and trace her lovely full mouth.

Because if he'd stayed in Marietta, he'd want to take her out to dinner just to see what she'd wear. He'd want to see how she'd do her hair. He'd want to make her laugh, she had such a lovely throaty laugh, and he'd wait for her smile, and the dimple that would flash. In his work, he created worlds and characters and he gave them a storyline and they followed it. He knew what would happen in advance. He had to. But with Amanda he didn't know what would happen, and it was exciting, and stimulating, as well as exasperating.

And just thinking about her, he pictured her at Rocco's in the dark peach dress with the tiny belt around her waist, and then of her on the path following the Marietta River, dressed in black and lavender, her long blonde ponytail swinging as she ran ahead of him, and then at Grey's with her sister, in a French blue cashmere sweater that hugged all of her curves a little too well, and made her eyes brighter, and richer, as if they were Montana sapphires.

She was pretty and smart and kind and funny… and she was most definitely a problem.

AMANDA TOLD HERSELF she was glad Tyler had left town. Good riddance, she'd added under her breath, as she turned off the lights in the salon for the night and dead-locked the front door.

But later on, upstairs in her apartment, she found herself thinking about him, and wondering why she felt empty and a little let down.

If she was truly glad he was gone, wouldn't she feel relief? Happiness? Freedom? Instead she sagged into her couch, unaccountably blue.

Charity arrived an hour later with a pizza, a bottle of red wine, and a big paper bag. While Amanda opened the wine, Charity dumped the paper bag onto the velvet covered ottoman that served as footstool and impromptu dining table. "Look what I found at the thrift store in Bozeman. Romance novels! Dozens of them."

Amanda smiled at the wash of pink and teal and purple covers on her ottoman as she handed Charity a glass of wine.

"How much were all of these?"

"Four for a dollar. I couldn't resist."

Amanda picked up one book with a cover featuring a handsome, elegantly dressed duke. It had been years since she'd actually sat and read a romance, too busy trying to get her salon going, too stressed by the constant financial worries of running her own business, never mind keeping her parents from financial disaster, because it seemed as if her parents *wanted* financial ruin. They had a history of making the worst decisions not just in Marietta, maybe in all of Montana.

She wouldn't say that her father had a gambling addiction, but he certainly lacked self-control when it came to making purchases that were not needed. Particularly purchases online, whether it be eBay, or any other Internet auction. He loved online auctions. He loved online shopping. He loved shopping off the TV. He loved small and medium packages arriving at the house. He felt like a victor... a winner... when he "won" an auction, somehow failing to put two and two together that he hadn't won anything, but rather he'd bought something, and he'd been the one who'd simply paid the most. He couldn't wrap his head around the fact that those endless, unnecessary purchases meant he was blowing his and Mom's meager income on silly things instead of necessities.

"I couldn't remember if you liked historicals or contemporaries better so I bought them all," Charity added, sipping her wine. "Let's divide the pile and then we'll switch—"

"I don't think I'm going to read them." Mandy dropped the book and sat down in a corner of the sofa, curling her legs under her. "There isn't time, and it's not the same anymore."

"What do you mean?"

"We're not going to meet men like that... handsome, successful, sexy... not here, not in Marietta."

"There are plenty of handsome men in Marietta!" Charity took another slow, thoughtful sip before casually adding, "Ty Justice."

"He's returned to Texas, and he doesn't count."

"Why not?"

"Because he's pompous and arrogant and makes far too many assumptions."

"Alpha heroes always do. Remember every Barbara Cartland we read? Arrogant, impossible, interfering aristocrat—"

"Tyler is not an aristocrat."

"But he's incredibly wealthy. He's mega rich."

"He isn't."

"He is. Look him up. In fact, let's Google him together."

"Let's not. And I don't want to discuss him anymore. Let's talk about the men who live *here*. The men who love Marietta. They're nice guys, but, face it, we've known them since we were in diapers. It's awfully hard to be excited about a man you've watched go through puberty and pimples."

"I don't even mind puberty and pimples. I just don't

want to be dragged out to a ranch. I want to find a great guy with a career in town as we both know I'm not cut out for country living."

"That's why you don't date cowboys."

"Exactly." Charity tucked long honey-blonde hair behind her ear. "But the cute ones do look so good in their Wranglers and boots—"

"You're cursing yourself, you know. You're destined to end up with a cowboy now."

"Only if I could be the *Cowboy Tycoon's Kidnapped Bride*."

"*No*. You would hate being kidnapped, much less to an isolated ranch. Texas ones might be different, but ours are muddy. They're not romantic. Stay in town. Much less dirt, and manure odors."

"Definitely don't like manure odor."

"I know."

"Maybe we should just eat pizza and stop talking."

"Good idea."

They got halfway through the pizza before calling it quits. Amanda topped off their wineglasses and curled back into the couch.

"Is it bad to want a tycoon?" Charity said after a moment, reaching for a faded, battered paperback, the book apparently well read, and much loved.

"I suppose it depends on why you want him."

"I just want a man who will love me, but also, make

things easier, not harder." She stared down at the book on her lap, studying the cover of the novel. "Men not like Dad," she added under her breath.

Mandy heard, though.

She lifted her head and looked at Charity, at the same moment Charity looked at her, and nothing else needed to be said because Amanda knew what Charity was thinking, just as Charity knew what Amanda was thinking.

"A man that can hold down a job, and not botch everything up because he can't stay sober." Charity's voice was rough with emotion. "A man with pride and self-respect who wouldn't dream of expecting his daughters to pay his bills because he'd rather drink than get sober."

Amanda closed her eyes, holding her breath, hating the wash of pain.

"I'm so angry he did that to you," Charity added quietly, fiercely. "I'm so mad that he nearly ruined everything for you."

Only Charity knew Mandy had destroyed her own credit last year, trying to help her parents when they couldn't pay their bills. Neither Charity nor Amanda had told Jenny, certain Jenny would feel obligated to rush in and help—again—and so Amanda decided she'd shoulder the responsibility this time, but it had cost her, dearly. If it wasn't for Bette, Amanda wouldn't have been able to close on her new salon.

"Dad has a problem," Amanda said after a moment.

"And Mom doesn't do anything about it."

"Mom's still afraid Dad might walk out."

"*Why?* That makes me crazy, because where would he go? What would he do? Mom takes care of everything for him. They're seriously dysfunctional."

"This is why Jenny insisted we go to college."

"And paid for our college."

"She didn't want us to end up without an education, or skills."

"She didn't want us to be Mom."

Charity returned the pink paperback to the ottoman. "That's sad."

And it was, Amanda thought, leaning forward to begin stacking the books into four tidy piles. Their mom had once been beautiful. She'd told her girls that in high school she'd won a modeling competition hosted by a local photographer and was told she had a bright future ahead of her, if she was willing to move to New York.

Apparently she wasn't, or couldn't, because two years later she was nineteen and pregnant with Jenny.

"I don't think we can look at it that way," Amanda said after a moment. "I think we have to be grateful Jenny was so level-headed and practical. If it weren't for her, neither of us would have gone to college. We wouldn't have thought it was possible. We wouldn't have thought *anything* was possible."

"Maybe Jenny was the smart one. She didn't read romances and she didn't daydream, and she didn't give in to fantasies about the way the world could be, and yet she still fell in love, and found her prince. He was from Marietta, too."

Mandy pushed the four piles together, making them one large square. "Maybe we need to leave Marietta."

"*What?*"

"I'm just beginning to think that we're never going to escape the past, or the names people used to call us."

"But that's all in the past!"

"Is it? Then why does Tyler Justice think I'm trying to take advantage of Bette?"

"He doesn't!"

"He does. He asked me if I knew her finances—"

"He didn't!"

"He *did*. And he hasn't put it in these exact words, but he seems to think I'm a manipulative gold digger—"

"If that's true, I won't want to be part of his fan club anymore. But are you sure he really thinks that, or are you possibly being a little sensitive?" Charity jumped from her seat onto the couch and wrapped her arms around her younger sister. "And I wouldn't blame you for being sensitive because you're as honest as they come, but he's an outsider and he doesn't know that."

"If Bette hadn't given me a loan, he'd respect my accomplishments," she answered darkly.

"I'm sure he respects what you've done. How can he not?

You've started your own business. You have all these truly fantastic ideas on how to expand it, and that takes guts, and vision. Jenny played it safe as a secretary, working for others. I've gone the same route. But you're doing your own thing and it's impressive, so don't let *anyone* make you feel inferior."

Charity's advice and pep talk was exactly what Amanda needed, but later that night, as Amanda struggled to fall asleep, she heard a little voice asking why did she care so much about Tyler's opinion in the first place?

Why should she care about what he thought?

The answer was so obvious, it annoyed her. She *liked* him, and not just a little, but the kind of attraction that made her feel fizzy and excited and a little breathless every time she was near him.

Just thinking about him now made her heart go faster.

Now if only he could see the best in her, not the worst.

THE WEEKEND ARRIVED, bringing with it beautiful weather, the temperature positively balmy for Montana for the last weekend of February. Amanda attended the early morning service at St. James and then returned home and changed and paid a visit to the local mercantile to buy paint.

Home again, she gave the charming picket fence in front of her house a fresh coat of white paint, and since she had the fence done by noon, she tackled the house, giving it a lovely, fresh coat of paint, too, because wasn't everything better when it was pink?

Charity, Sadie, and Tricia all joined her after lunch, and then Sadie's husband, Rory, came over when he realized Sadie was on a tall ladder, trying to paint the second floor. Rory made a few calls and by midafternoon he had a half dozen cowboy friends showing up with paint brushes, and the entire house was completed by dinner.

While Amanda cleaned all the brushes, Charity called a to-go order into the Chinese restaurant for dinner for twelve, and Tricia went to pick up plastic cups and wine, and they all ate sitting on the front porch and in folding chairs in the lawn, as twilight turned to dusk and then the dark lavender blue of night. She turned on her porch lights and the fairy lights she strung in her trees year round, and returned to her folding chair, now bundled in a winter coat, she kept smiling at her pink house with the soft aqua front door.

It was outrageous, and rather shocking, but it was also fun, and it'd be beautiful come summer when all the lavender bushes bloomed.

Maybe this would be the year her climbing roses took off. And maybe she could find some clematis that would flower, too.

Maybe tough alpha men wouldn't really hate a pink Barbie dream house.

Shifting in her folding chair, she lifted her plastic tumbler, and toasted her friends. "Thank you, everyone, for pitching in today. I really, really appreciate you. It wouldn't have happened without you."

"That might have been a good thing," one of Rory's cowboy friends teased from the back.

Charity made a face. "I love the pink house," she said to Amanda, "and most of all, I love you."

Amanda blew her sister a kiss and, tipping her head back, studied her house. She felt full of so many emotions, most good, but also a tiny bit wistful. Today was pretty much perfect. The only thing that could have made it better was having Tyler here, and seeing more of her world. She suspected, though, that if he was here, he wouldn't have been supportive of the paint job, never mind being part of the painting party, and the painting party was what made her love Marietta so very much. Here, people helped people. Even when it meant turning a perfectly respectable white house rose.

MONDAY MORNING TYLER woke to a text from the CEO of TexTron. In a bid to placate an angry board, he'd made the difficult decision to sell the entire entertainment division. The entertainment division was likely to be broken up in the sale, with different arms of the division going to different buyers. The CEO had been approached a month ago with an offer from a company interested in acquiring Justice Games, offering a significant amount of money and the CEO planned on accepting the offer today, which meant that Tyler was free to move on to different things.

Tyler reread the text in bed, and then headed to the kitchen to make coffee, and read it again.

He called his CEO but his call went straight to voicemail. "Bill, it's Tyler. Got your message but I'm unclear about a few things. Call me."

Bill didn't return the call for almost an hour. By then, Tyler had several cups of coffee and more time to process the news, but not enough time to process his shock or disbelief.

"That's it?" Tyler said, when Bill called. "I'm just... done?"

"They want the games, Tyler. They don't want you."

"Why?"

"You know why. They're going to want to change things, and you wouldn't be good with that. You're protective of your games—"

"Absolutely."

"But they want to make money, not protect your creative integrity."

"They're going to destroy Justice Games."

"They're going to be giving us—and you—a great deal of money. You could retire off this, live a comfortable life. It's a win-win for everyone."

"Not for me. And not for those that love my games."

"I love your passion, Tyler, I do. But that's the piece that has always held you back. You still think with your heart, not your head. Justice Games is just a revenue stream for us, and it's going to be a revenue stream for Sheenan Media."

Sheenan Media. Tyler knew that name. It rang more than a few bells, but didn't know why. "Is that the company that you're selling my company to?"

"Justice Games hasn't been your company for over two years now. You don't work for yourself. You work for us."

"You promised me control when I sold Justice Games to you. You assured me I would remain at the helm."

"For as long as we owned the company, yes. But we're selling—"

"I want to buy it back."

"I've already accepted their offer."

"Change your mind. I'll pay you more than whatever they offered."

"They're paying me cash, and I doubt you have that kind of liquidity. We close by the end of this week. I'm sorry, Tyler, it's essentially a done deal. I'll have Jess pack up your office and drive everything to you this afternoon. Better not to have you in the office. There is no point in upsetting your team." Bill hesitated. "Let me say that another way. You cannot mention this to your team. They work for me, not you."

"And if I came up with the cash? What then?"

"I still wouldn't sell to you. I made a deal, and I'm not going to pull out now. It'd be disastrous for our reputation."

TYLER WAS TWENTY minutes into his run when he realized why he recognized the Sheenan name.

Troy Sheenan.

Troy was big in the Bay Area in high tech. Tyler had met him at a number of charity events, those black tie affairs where everyone was committed to doing good and giving back. Someone had introduced the two of them, casually remarking that both had ties to Montana. "My father's from there," Tyler had said.

"Mine, too," Troy answered with a smile. "And maybe that's why we're both here in California."

As Tyler ran, he played the conversation over in his head, a conversation that had taken place years ago. Six or seven years, maybe more.

Was Troy behind the buy-out?

Back home, Tyler showered, changed into comfortable Levi's and a soft hoodie, better for sitting down at his desk to do some research.

But when he typed in Troy Sheenan, and Sheenan Industries, he didn't just pull up Troy, but links to a Cormac Sheenan, founder of Sheenan Media.

Sheenan Media. There it was.

Tyler clicked on a link to Sheenan Media and it led him to the landing page for the company's website, based out of—wait for it—Marietta, Montana.

Impossible.

He leaned back, and shook his head as he continued to

read. The West Coast media conglomerate only recently relocated all corporate offices to the hometown of company founder, Cormac Sheenan.

It didn't take a lot more research to discover that Cormac was the younger brother of Troy Sheenan, and older brother of *New York Times* bestselling crime author, Sean S. Finley, and Austin bio-tech brain, Dillion Sheenan.

Interesting family. The Sheenans seemed to be everywhere. High-tech, bio-tech, media, publishing. And it all started in Crawford County, Montana.

Tyler turned off his computer and pushed away from his desk. It looked like he was going back to Marietta sooner than he expected.

BY TUESDAY, MARIETTA'S lovely unseasonably warm weather was gone, chased away by a new cold front that had dropped temperatures by thirty degrees. Amanda had to crank up the heater in the salon that morning, especially as she knew Bette was coming for her usual Tuesday appointment and Bette had a tendency to get chilly.

Bette was quiet, though, during her appointment, and missing her usual sparkle.

"Are you feeling alright?" Amanda asked, concerned.

"Just worried about Tyler," she answered.

"I honestly can't see him making you move if you don't want to."

"Oh, it's not that. I think something has happened. I'm not sure what it is, but he sounded rather despondent on the phone when we spoke Monday. He was not at all like himself."

"Maybe he'd had a stressful day."

"Maybe." Bette fidgeted with the strap of her purse resting in her lap. She never liked to hang her purse up on the hook, preferring to keep it on her lap. "He said he's coming back to Marietta. Should be here this weekend."

Amanda froze, comb hovering midair. "That soon?"

"I know. That was my first thought, too. Why so soon?"

"Maybe he misses all of our snow and ice."

"Or our wind."

"The wind is delightful."

They smiled at each other in the mirror, and for a moment the mood lightened, but then Bette's smile slipped, and faded. "I don't want to be a worrywart, but I think something's happened. Call it female intuition, or grandmother ESP, but something has happened and I don't think it's good."

"Well, knowing you, you'll soon get to the bottom of whatever it is, and then, knowing you, you'll know exactly how to make everything better."

AMANDA COULDN'T STOP thinking about Tyler, and how he was returning to Marietta, and she knew it wasn't smart to feel so hopeful, but that was exactly how she felt. Hopeful and excited.

He made her want more again, not in terms of work, but in terms of dating and relationships. He made her want to be in a relationship. He made her imagine how wonderful it would be to have a boyfriend again and someone who cared about her day, and someone who'd dress up and take her to dinner, someone who'd think a movie night sounded romantic, someone who'd hold her hand, and kiss her good night.

Someone who'd love her.

Someone who'd be proud of her.

Someone who'd celebrate her successes and encourage her when everything seemed to go wrong.

And she wanted someone she could be there for, too.

Her sisters and friends were wonderful, but having that special guy, would be wonderful, too.

Someone who might one day be the "one." The one who'd put a tux on and marry her in front of a hundred guests. The one who'd want to start a family with her and cared so much for her that he wanted to be there to grow old with her.

She'd kind of given those dreams up, and had focused her energy and attention on her business, but suddenly Tyler had her thinking again and dreaming again...

She tried to rein in her imagination and heart, knowing she was just asking to be disappointed, and not even sure how everything had gotten so out of hand in the first place. He lived out of town. He thought the worst of her. Why would she be thinking of him all the time?

Was it because she loved Bette?

Or was there something else, something bigger, something deeper that was pulling her to him?

Either way, she'd know soon enough because, from the sound of things, Tyler would be back in just days.

WHEN HE LEFT Marietta last week, Tyler had promised his grandmother he'd be back within two weeks. Instead, he was back just a week later. Crazy how things worked.

He left the Bozeman airport in his rental car, a big four wheel drive SUV this time as he planned on doing some exploring while in Montana. On reaching Marietta, he took a drive down Main Street, and then a detour past the Wright Salon on his way to his grandmother's. He'd only meant to drive past. Instead he found himself braking hard in the middle of Church Street.

She'd done it.

She'd painted the house pink. Bubble gum, cotton-candy-pink.

He frowned, and then sighed, and then laughed, because the house was now a Pepto-pink monstrosity. All she needed to do now was hang a sparkly unicorn flag, or perhaps plant some plastic flamingos in the barren front yard, to confirm her insanity.

And yet, her insanity suddenly appealed to him. He had to give her points for being original. He admired her style. It might not be the smartest business decision, but at least she was true to herself.

Still smiling, still shaking his head, he continued on to Gram's on Bramble, but his smile faded as he parked his car in front of her house.

He wasn't looking forward to telling her he'd lost his company, but far better she heard the news from him, than some cynical outside source.

It didn't take long to break the news to her, either.

"I'm unemployed, Gram. I'm sorry," he told his grandmother, as they sat at her dining room table having milk and apple pie twenty minutes later.

He was touched that she'd gone to the trouble of picking up his favorite pie from Main Street Diner, because there was nothing like a perfectly spiced, homemade apple pie when his world felt out of kilter.

"Were you fired?" Gram asked bluntly.

"No. Worse. My company was sold."

"But I thought your company had already been sold."

"It had, two years ago. I sold it to TexTron, but then they turned around and sold it to a media conglomerate and the new company doesn't want me. They just want the games."

"I see."

"And now I am without a job."

"I'm sure you'll get another one. You'll land on your feet, my dear. I have confidence in you."

He checked his smile. "Thank you, Gram. I appreciate that."

"And if you're worrying about money—"

"I'm not."

"I can float you a loan. Just to get you by."

"Gram, I'm not short of cash."

"Did they give you severance pay?"

"Something like that."

"I hope they gave you your vacation time and things like that."

"They did."

"Well, you can stay here for as long as you want. I have plenty of rooms, and this is a big house, there's lots of space. There is no reason we can't be good housemates, provided you pick up after yourself and all." She frowned. "You don't leave your things lying around, do you? I can't imagine you would. Your father was very tidy himself. But then, your grandfather Justice wouldn't have permitted Patrick to just drop things willy-nilly. He was a military man. Everything had a time and place."

"I'm not a slob, no." He leaned forward and kissed his grandmother on the cheek. "Now let me take care of these dishes and then I think I'm going to change and go for a quick run before it's dark."

"A run now? After pie?"

"Well, that way I can have more pie later, right?" He grinned and rose, taking the dishes with him.

"What about dinner?" she called.

He returned to the dining room, and leaned against the doorframe. "Would you mind if I skipped dinner tonight? There are some things I need to do."

"Like what?"

"Companies in the area I wanted to check out."

"Oh."

"You sound disappointed."

"I thought you were maybe going to stop by and see Mandy."

"I might, but I might not. Why?"

"Because you want to see if I've given her any more of my things?"

"*Gram.*"

"I can't think what you possibly have to say to her. You've said enough, I believe."

"Why do you say that?"

"I know more than you'd like me to know—"

"Amanda said something."

"Amanda said nothing. But others did. You've gone and made a mess out of things, and that wasn't necessary. So do us both a favor, and stay away from her. You haven't been very kind to her."

"I sincerely regret it if that is the case."

"It's the case."

"I'll apologize to her."

"Take her flowers first. Before you ask her to dinner."

"Gram."

"Really pretty ones. This isn't the time to be shabby."

CHAPTER SEVEN

"**Y**OUR SEXY GAME developer is back in town," Charity said nonchalantly late Thursday afternoon as Amanda placed the last foil in her hair and set the timer.

"I don't have a sexy game developer," Amanda answered, wiping her hands on a small towel gathering her combs and color bowls.

"I'm sorry, should I have called him a designer?"

"The point is, he's not mine."

"But he certainly seems interested in you."

"He isn't."

"How can you say that when he's here with the biggest bouquet of flowers I've ever seen?"

Amanda turned around and, yes, he was talking to Emily at the front desk, holding a massive bouquet of pink tulips and roses and other gorgeous flowers, all pink as well.

For a split second she was tempted to run to the back and hide. And then he was approaching her and it was too late to run.

"Hi," he said.

"Hello," she answered, shifting the plastic color bowls,

feeling as awkward as a schoolgirl. "You're back already."

"I am."

"Missed Montana?"

"Not Montana, just Marietta."

"It's an addictive little town."

His lips curved into a crooked smile. "You warned me."

Everything inside her seemed to light up, or was that the effect of her mad, galloping pulse? "I did."

"These are for you. I do believe you like everything pink."

She juggled the bowls again and accepted the flowers. "As long as I'm not wearing it."

He smiled, creases fanning from the corners of his eyes. "But you have no problem with a pink house."

"No. I think the house loves it."

"She does look younger."

Amanda laughed out loud, and then remembering her sister in the chair behind her, glanced back at Charity who was grinning from ear to ear, looking an awful lot like the Cheshire cat.

"Ty, you remember my sister, Charity? Charity, say hello to Tyler while I go put these gorgeous flowers in a vase." And then she went to the kitchen to find a vase and try to pull herself together because her heart was pounding and her skin was tingling and she felt far too giddy and excited.

She shouldn't be so excited.

She shouldn't feel as if something amazing had just happened. And yet when he'd handed her the flowers, and he'd made the joke about the house looking younger, she'd felt a bubble of pleasure, the kind of pleasure that was very close to joy. It was impossible, really, to feel this kind of happiness. It didn't make sense. He didn't make sense. And yet everything in her wanted to rush back out and see him, and talk to him, but the sheer intensity of her emotions made her hold back.

"Maybe I should have bought a vase with the flowers." Tyler was standing just inside the kitchen, looking out of place in all the white paint and Victorian details.

"I love the flowers, and I have plenty of vases." She opened the cupboard door beneath the sink, revealing an assortment of glass containers. She reached for a cranberry-pink vase. "I think this will be perfect."

She felt him watching her as she filled the vase, and then trimmed the stems and put them in water, fussing with some of the flowers, arranging them to better advantage.

"What do you think?" she said, stepping back.

"Beautiful."

She flashed him a smile. "I think so, too. Thank you."

"I'm sorry about… everything… before. I didn't mean to imply that you weren't trustworthy. I just worry about Gram, maybe because my dad used to worry about her. She's been taken advantage of before—"

"I'd never do that to her, or anyone." She looked away, out the window where darkness had fallen, hiding the world. "I grew up without a lot, raised by parents who lived constantly on the brink of financial disaster. My sisters and I are always trying to bail them out of trouble. It was my turn last time to help, and it… just backfired. It blew up on me, and hurt me financially. That's where your grandmother stepped in, and she saved me. She did. But it was really uncomfortable accepting help from her. I didn't want her help. I like to be able to do things myself. I need to be able to take care of myself. I value independence and admire self-sufficiency. In others and myself."

"I'm sorry—"

"No. Don't be sorry. I'm glad you're looking out for Bette. She needs you. She needs to have someone who loves her, dearly."

"I think you love her."

"But isn't it even better when you have lots of people love you?"

"Yes," he said quietly.

Something in his gaze made her warm, and then hot. She found herself looking at his lovely firm mouth and wondering how he kissed, and just imagining kissing him made the narrow kitchen feel smaller, and a little too intimate. Thankfully the timer on her phone pinged, forcing her to action.

"I need to check Charity's color," she said huskily.

"I know it's last minute, but have dinner with me tomorrow. We can try those margaritas at Rosita's. What do you say?"

There was no way she could say no. It was what she'd

been wanting ever since he left. A proper night out, just the two of them together. "Yes."

AFTER WORK FRIDAY, Amanda showered and changed into on one of her favorite dresses, another Charity design, which was probably a knock-off of a true vintage dress. It was navy, with a slightly asymmetrical neckline in cream, with three-quarter sleeves, and narrow cream cuffs. The bodice was fitted, accenting her shape, and the skirt fell to her calves, long and full. The skirt did a little swing as she walked, and she paired it with her best navy heels for a little extra pizazz. She parted her hair on the side and teased the crown for a little height, before pulling it into a high ponytail.

Tyler had insisted on picking her up and he was out front exactly on time. Glad she was ready, she slipped on her coat and gloves before going down to meet him.

He was out of the car the moment she emerged from the house. He gave her a dazzling smile as she approached the car. "You're beautiful."

The compliment caught her off guard and her face grew warm. "Thank you."

They were seated immediately at Rosita's and Tyler asked the waitress to recommend her favorite margarita, and she did, saying it was their Cadillac margarita, top shelf tequila, and hand shaken. "I have to try it," he said.

"Me, too," Amanda agreed.

They ordered the nachos and then sipped their drinks, which were amazing, and in between bites of nachos, Tyler told her that there had been changes at work and he was still trying to process it all. "The bottom line, though, is that Gram won't let me stay at the Graff anymore. She says she won't accept the excuse that I need the business center."

"She does have Internet," Amanda said, smiling.

"And a small printer in the guest room."

"Your grandmother is practical."

"And smart. She's outmaneuvered me."

"You don't reach eighty without having some game."

He laughed. "Gram does have game, doesn't she?"

"Don't let her sweet smile and innocent expression fool you."

"As long as she's not worrying about me. I'm okay, in every way."

Amanda reached for a tortilla chip covered with cheese. "She was worried earlier in the week, but I think she likes to worry about you. It gives her a sense of purpose."

"I don't want to create stress for her."

"She's so happy to have you here," she answered, popping the chip in her mouth.

He was silent a moment. "She is happy, isn't she?"

Amanda finished chewing and swallowing and brushed her fingers off. "She's gone a long time without family close."

"Which is why she's made friends her family." His brow furrowed. "She needs family."

"She's a lover, not a fighter."

"I can picture her in boxing gloves, though. She'd fight if she had to."

"Absolutely. Your grandmother is no pushover."

He smiled and then his smile faded and he looked away, gaze focused on the mural on the wall. "I've been so immersed in my work for the past few years that I've been pretty distant. Not fair to her."

"She's never complained. She's only ever talked about how wonderful you are, and clever, and hardworking. She always lights up when she talks about you, and I'm not saying that to make you feel better, it's the truth. Your grandmother doesn't sit around feeling sorry for herself. She's not morose, or lonely, but would she like more time with you? Absolutely. But does that mean she has to leave all of her friends here... friends who have become her family? I hope not."

He was silent for a moment. "Remember I said there were changes at work? They were pretty life changing actually. My company was sold. I'm... free."

"Free?"

"Have no commitments."

She set her margarita glass down. "Explain this to me."

"TexTron is selling off its entertainment division, and Justice Games was the first to go. Apparently there was an interested buyer, a company who'd already made an offer some time ago, and the CEO of TexTron accepted it." He nudged his goblet. "I have to admit, I'm having a hard time with it. I wasn't ready to lose it all."

"You had no idea this was in the works?"

"None at all."

"What does it mean for you financially?"

"I'm good. I'm great. I made some significant money from the sale, but Justice Games was more than a financial return. It was my… baby. My passion. Even though that is such a corny word and I cringe saying it."

She felt for him, she did. "My salon is my passion."

"Yes, but you are a gorgeous woman and you can say things like that. Men aren't supposed to have 'passions.' We're supposed to be strong. Tough. Rugged—" He broke off as she began to laugh. "What?"

"Don't look so offended. I'm not laughing at you. Honest. I just find it rather sweet, that's all."

"Sweet?"

"Of course, your work is your passion! Why else would you do it? And how is it emasculating being committed to your work?"

"I thought I'd have three more years in Texas, at least three, because part of the purchase was that I remain at the helm, and then once the five year clause elapsed, I'd be free. But suddenly I'm free now. The sale of Justice Games cuts me loose."

"Do you regret selling Justice Games?"

He nodded.

His faint nod spoke volumes, and she felt for him. She really did. She couldn't imagine her world without her salon and clients. It gave her life purpose and meaning. "So what now?" she asked.

"I don't know—" He broke off. "Actually I do know," he said more firmly. "I plan to approach the head of the company that bought Justice Games and convince him to sell it back to me."

"What if he won't?"

"Then I'll convince him he needs me."

She was silent a moment. "Not to be devil's advocate, but what if he doesn't need you? What then?"

"I'll start a new company. Create new games."

"Why not just do that now?"

"Because I like the company I built. And, the new media conglomerate that bought Justice Games is right here in Marietta."

Her eyes widened. "What?"

He drew a slow breath, before asking, "How familiar are you with the Sheenan family?"

"Very familiar. I never went to school with any of them, but both my sisters did. Charity was a year behind Dillon, the youngest of the Sheenans, but they were both in high school at the same time, and Jenny knew Cormac, Trey, and Troy."

"Wow." He leaned back in his seat.

She arched a brow. "Wow, what?"

"You really do know them."

"Again, I don't know them well. I know their wives better. They all come to me for their hair. Cormac, too."

"What's he like? Cormac?"

She pictured the only blond Sheenan and gave a little shrug. "He's probably the hardest to get to know. He's quiet, self-contained. I've heard others describe him as arrogant, but I don't think that's fair. He doesn't wear his heart on his sleeve, but he's incredibly loyal to his family and friends. Last year his company was named the best place to work in Park, Gallatin, and Crawford Counties—" She broke off, looked up at him. "Why are you asking?"

"Sheenan Media bought Justice Games."

Her mouth opened a little, then closed. That was a game changer. "I don't—" She broke off, shook her head. "Never mind."

"What?"

"I shouldn't say anything. I don't know—"

"Just tell me what you're thinking."

"Cormac Sheenan wouldn't buy your company just to turn it around and sell it back to you. Knowing him, he's not looking to make money off a quick sell. He doesn't need the money. Cormac is always about strategy. If he's bought it from TexTron, he has plans for it."

"I'm not giving up without a fight."

She was silent a long moment. "Do you want me to introduce you to him?"

"No. But thank you. I have a call with him already scheduled for Monday."

"Keep me posted."

"I will." And then he smiled faintly. "But if things work the way I think they do in Marietta, you might know the outcome before even I do."

THE NEXT MORNING Amanda rolled out of bed and went straight to the window to get a look at the sky. The horizon was clear at the moment but a cold front was moving in today, disaster for special events like weddings and outdoor photo shoots, which was what was on Amanda's schedule for the day.

She'd been booked for the McInnes wedding months ago, with her scheduled to do the entire wedding party's hair and makeup, beginning with the mother of the bride at eight thirty, and then the mother of the groom at nine thirty, with the bridesmaids and bride to follow, until everyone was ready for the photo shoot at Miracle Lake before the five o'clock ceremony at the gorgeous Emerson Barn in Paradise Valley. Amanda had scheduled two additional stylists to work with her for hair since the bridal party had grown from four bridesmaids to six, and one flower girl to three, but only Amanda would go on location for the photos and then the ceremony.

After nine years as a hair stylist, Amanda had done the

hair and makeup for dozens and dozens of Montana brides, and there were two things every bride wanted on her wedding day—her groom and good weather. But in Montana, good weather was never a sure thing, much less the first weekend in March.

As expected, heavy gray clouds gathered all morning, the clouds hanging low in the sky, promising snow. The snow held off, though, until early afternoon when Brooke, the bride-to-be, was finally the one in Amanda's chair.

"You're going to get beautiful photos," Amanda said as she finished sliding another pin into the updo that looked effortlessly chic and elegant but had taken an hour to create. "And with luck, it might not even snow until later tonight."

Brooke flashed her phone. "The weather channel said it's supposed to start snowing in the next hour."

Amanda checked to see if the style was secure and then reached for another pin. "And if it does, all that white will make a perfect backdrop—"

"But you won't see my dress against the snow. I'll just be a blob of white."

"Your skin will look luminous and your gown is that of a royal princess. It's going to be magical. Trust me."

"My bridesmaids are in purple."

"They'll gleam in the snow, especially when you do your pictures in front of Miracle Lake."

Brooke blinked back tears. "This is so stressful."

"Don't let it be."

"We don't have weather like this in California. It's almost always sunny in Newport. I wish we were in California now."

"Well, true, but Scott is a rancher here, and you love Scott. You said he's your best friend and he makes you happier than you've ever been."

"He does, and he is. And I don't hate Montana, but everyone was saying it was going to be gorgeous this weekend. Unusually warm. Spring-like."

"Montana weather is notoriously fickle, and unpredictable. The moment they say good weather, brace yourself for wind and rain."

Brooke glanced out the salon window, up at the dark sky. "Or snow."

"It'll still be beautiful… maybe even more beautiful."

"Promise?"

"Promise."

"And you'll be there for the photos at Miracle Lake and Emerson Barn? And you'll stay until I walk down the aisle?"

"You invited me to stay for the whole dang thing. I believe I RSVPed yes, too."

"Yes, you did. I'll see you soon?"

"I'm right behind you. I just need to pack up my things and I'm on my way."

But fifteen minutes later Amanda was still in Marietta, trying to find a ride out of town as her car refused to start, and the RV, which would be perfect for today's location shoot, was still not running.

Amanda dashed back into the salon, shivering. "Emily, can I borrow your car? Mine won't start and Brooke is expecting me at Miracle Lake any minute for her photo shoot."

"Mandy, I'd give you my car if I had it, but Mitch dropped me off today. He had to go to Missoula and didn't trust his car, not with the possibility of snow later."

Amanda glanced at the sky which seemed to grow darker by the moment. "I'm praying there won't be snow."

"It's inevitable."

"Grr." She bit her lip, knowing she had to get there. "What about the other girls? Anyone have a car today?"

"Tamara drove but she's got her son's basketball game in a bit and driving kids."

"That's right. I'll just call Charity. If she's parked down-town, I could just run and grab it."

But Charity didn't pick up. "I'll try Bette," she said, hanging up.

"Or maybe Bette's grandson. He has an SUV rental, and we all know he's back in town." Emily paused. "And he's really hot."

"He's Bette's grandson. And he's not *that* hot."

"You get totally flustered every time he's around. Which means you think he's really hot."

"You have no idea what you're talking about."

"I've worked with you for almost four years. You had

dinner with him last night. *And* he's the first man that makes you blush and giggle—"

"It was really more like drinks last night, and I do not giggle."

"And you better call him, or I will."

"You don't have his number."

Emily typed on the keyboard and read his number off the screen. "I have everyone's numbers. It's my job."

Amanda groaned. "Okay, read me his number. But he doesn't make me giggle."

TYLER WAS AT the salon in minutes. Amanda had everything by the front door and raced out when she spotted the black SUV pulling up in front of the salon. She carried her makeup and hair kits, while Emily carried out her dress and shoes for the wedding since she was staying. Amanda didn't know how she'd get home yet but was certain there would be a familiar guest who could drop her off afterward.

"You really don't mind giving me a ride?" Amanda asked breathlessly as she slid into the passenger seat. "It's going to be a good twenty-minute drive there, and then if you wait during photos, another hour on top."

"I don't mind waiting. I have nothing else to do."

"Maybe just drop me off and you could come back—"

"I'm not going to leave you on the side of Copper Mountain."

"It wouldn't be on the side, it'd be at the lake."

And just then, the first flakes began to fall, small, light white bits falling from the sky. Soon it was falling harder, a steady curtain of white. Amanda frowned at the view out the windshield. "I'd told Brooke that there wouldn't be too much, but it's coming down."

"Can you change the location for the shoot?"

"I'll ask when we get there."

Amanda's phone rang just then. She answered, thinking it was Brooke, and she was right. "We're almost there, and I was going to ask you that very thing. We don't have to do the outdoor shots—"

"Scott thinks this is great," Brooke interrupted hoarsely. "He's enjoying this, and thinks we should at least try to get some shots in the snow. But he's wearing a suit jacket. The girls are wearing a little bit of silk and that's it."

"Then we'll just shoot the boys at the lake, and we'll do the girls at Emerson's barn."

Brooke was silent a moment. "Do you really think the pictures would be pretty at the lake? With the snow?"

"I think if you didn't freeze to death, it'd be gorgeous."

"Should we go for it?"

"We can try, and the moment you're miserable, we'll pack up and head to the barn. See you soon. We're almost there."

Miracle Lake was a favorite spot for ice skaters in the winter, as well as an excellent place to hike and picnic in the summer. But today, in early March, the road leading to the lake was deserted except for the handful of cars for the wedding party. The branches of the big evergreens lining the road looked frosted, while the low clouds hid the peak of Copper Mountain.

"Where is the lake?" Tyler asked, parking in the spot Amanda indicated.

"Over there," she said gesturing toward a meadow. "We've got to walk down that little slope to get there."

"All the girls are walking down that slope in dresses and high heels?"

"I'm hoping they've changed to cowboy boots. That had been the plan."

"She's right. They will freeze."

"Hoping we can get a couple quick, fun shots and then pack up. In Marietta, we do a lot of brides in snow pictures. Winter weddings are becoming increasingly popular."

She climbed out of his SUV and opened the back to collect her makeup box kit and tote bag with hair styling products.

"The dress?" he asked, gesturing to the hanger.

"For later when I transform from hired help to favored guest."

"Got it." He closed the back of the car and took the kit from her. "Lead the way."

She opened her mouth to protest because no one ever carried her things for her. "You don't have to carry my stuff."

"I know."

Her gaze met his and held for a beat.

She frowned, a little befuddled, not quite knowing what to do with him, or how to think of him. He wasn't the enemy anymore. And he wasn't a boyfriend. And they weren't dating, so what was he? Because he was something... most definitely something. Every time he was near, her heart beat a little faster and she felt so sensitive, her skin hot and prickly, her insides churning with nerves. No one flustered her, but he did. He made her feel sixteen, and as excited as she'd been at her first prom.

She mustered a smile. "Let's do this."

Unfortunately, the wedding photographer, Ted, wasn't from Montana, but a friend of the family's from Southern California, and Amanda suspected he was far less experienced than Brooke knew, because even though he'd arrived with cameras and meters and a plethora of lenses, he wasn't at all prepared for the cold, icy conditions at the lake, and Ted struggled to get going, spending most of his time frowning at his screen.

Amanda stood off to the side, chewing the inside of her lip, worrying that Brooke and the girls were slowly turning to ice sculptures while Ted changed lenses yet again.

"Ted, what's wrong?" Brooke called, teeth chattering, her six bridesmaids huddling around her like forlorn sheep, while their elaborate hairstyles sagged beneath the accumulating snow.

Amanda dashed over to the girls to deal with hair while Ted struggled to give Brooke a satisfactory answer.

"I'm just…" Ted said, and then sighed. "It's just… the cold. The camera is fogging. It'll be okay."

"Alright."

But Ted's confidence seemed to be struggling, and Amanda told jokes to make the girls smile and laugh, hating to see them shivering in a miserable clump in front of the lake which had never looked more atmospheric with wispy clouds rising up off the surface and steady lacy flakes falling from the sky.

"You don't have to do this," Amanda reminded Brooke.

Brooke glanced toward her groom, Scott, who was flinging snowballs with his groomsmen. "They're having fun."

"They're boys. What do you expect? Next thing you know they'll be making snow angels."

Brooke laughed, just as Amanda had intended, but Amanda was concerned. Ted needed to figure it out soon. She had to bite her lip to keep from giving the photographer direction, and Ted wasn't soothing anyone's frayed nerves by muttering about oceans and sunsets and snow not being his thing. Just when Amanda didn't think she could handle it a moment longer, she saw Tyler approach Ted.

The whole bridal party watched as Tyler spoke to the photographer, but Tyler's voice was pitched low so Amanda couldn't hear what was being said. After a moment Ted's tense expression eased, and he handed his camera to Tyler.

Tyler looked through the viewfinder and then said something to Ted. Ted nodded, and adjusted something on his camera, and then they talked a little more and then Ted called out to Brooke, "Brooke, lift your flowers to your nose. Yes, just like that. Smell them. Nice. And now, bridesmaids, put Brooke in the middle, three girls on each side, and can you all walk toward me? Don't look at me. Look at Brooke and each other. Just be natural and smile and have a good time. Forget I'm here."

The bride and bridesmaids all had bare shoulders and their cheeks were glowing pink, but they did as Ted asked, talking and walking and laughing around their chattering teeth even as their boots sank into the powdery snow.

"That's great," Ted called. "Love it. How about we get a shot of those cowboy boots? Girls, all flowers to the left hand, lift your skirts up with the right hand. Nice! Now put your right boot forward, point the toes, maybe a little can-can kick. Fantastic."

Ted snapped away, and then glanced down at his camera to check the images. He showed them to Tyler, and Tyler smiled and clapped Ted on the shoulder before leaving the photographer to do his job.

"What did you say to him?" Amanda said to Tyler as he joined her beneath a cluster of trees that she was using for shelter.

"To overexpose. Photographing snow is notoriously tricky because you can't get a mid-tone for your meter, so he needed to set it to +2 to keep his shots from being so blue-gray. And once he adjusted his settings and focused on the pops of color out there—the bride's bouquet, the bridesmaids' purple gowns—the photos stopped looking so monotone. All the flat gray was rattling him, but he's sorted it out now."

"How did you know what to tell him? About shooting in snow?"

"I grew up doing a lot of snowboarding, and during college I got into extreme sports photography. Helped pay for bills, and let me travel at the same time."

"How did you get into 'extreme sports photography'? That's not something you just get into, is it?"

"I took a video camera and began filming, and then went home and learned how to edit. The early stuff was pretty raw, but I got better over time."

She was impressed. "That's cool," she said, looking at him with fresh appreciation.

"Have I finally done something to impress you?" he teased, his green gaze locking with hers, his gaze so focused and intense that she grew warm and rather breathless.

He was *not* innocent. He knew exactly what he was doing with that look of his. Tyler was dangerous for her self-control.

"Amanda!" Brooke shouted, interrupting the moment. "Help! I think I've smudged my lipstick!"

Amanda flashed Tyler a wry smile. "That's my cue."

While Amanda touched up Brooke and the bridesmaids' hair and makeup a second time, Ted photographed the groom and the groomsmen. Some of the braver guys were still throwing snowballs, and pelting each other fairly hard, too.

"This is nuts," Brooke said, sniffling, watching them with a crooked smile.

"This is Montana," Amanda answered, giving Brooke's wayward curl a little tug, drawing it back so that it wouldn't fall in her eyes, but off to the side to frame her face.

"You're a native, aren't you?"

"How can you tell?"

"You seem to relish the cold and snow."

"I wouldn't say I relish it, but I've just grown up in it. It wouldn't be March without snow and ice. Or April. Or possibly May."

"Stop it!"

Amanda brushed tiny flakes off the tip of Brooke's pink nose and then another smattering of flakes from her cheeks. "We had snow Memorial Day weekend a few years back."

"Scott didn't tell me any of this." Brooke stomped her feet to keep warm. "What about your boyfriend? Is he a native, too?"

"My boyfriend?"

"Over there. Tyler. Isn't that his name?"

"Yes. But, no, he's not my boyfriend. He's just in town visiting, and we're just friends."

Brooke arched a dark brown eyebrow. "I don't think so. He really likes you."

"No."

"Have you ever seen the way he looks at you?"

"Nope, and Brooke, I think you're good to go!"

But Brook didn't budge. "He looks at you the way I look at meringues. Delicious."

Amanda rolled her eyes. "Hardly, and Ted's calling you. Time for pictures with your man before you all turn to icicles."

"But Tyler is staying for the wedding today, right? You're both staying for the ceremony and reception. There's a place for you at dinner, at the reception."

"I'm staying. Tyler is just dropping me off."

"You have a plus one."

"I didn't RSVP for one."

"I gave you one. You have to have a plus one, and he's yours." Brooke gave her a little squeeze. "And you can't say no because it's my special day." She flashed Amanda a triumphant grin before lifting her full white skirts to march back through the snow to Ted and her groom.

PICTURES OVER, TYLER picked up Amanda's oversized makeup kit and carried it back to his car while she spoke to Ted about the pictures at Emerson Barn. The bridal party returned to their cars lining the road, they were shivering, and teeth chattering, but also laughing and teasing each other. He was glad to see that they were all in good spirits. The photo shoot had been frigid but fun and it had most definitely "broken the ice."

Inside his SUV, he turned on the car and cranked up the heat so that it'd be warm for Amanda when she arrived. She opened the door a few minutes later and climbed inside, and sighed with pleasure at the warmth. "This feels so good!" She rubbed her hands and held them in front of the heater vents.

She was wearing black leggings and snow boots and a fitted black parka with a beige knit cap on top of her long blonde hair. The cap had a huge pom-pom at the end and with her pink cheeks, pink nose, and bright eyes, she looked ridiculously cute.

"I think I was picturing something much bigger."

"Your parents never brought you when you visited your grandparents?"

"We didn't ever visit."

"At all?"

"Dad didn't have good memories of Montana."

"That's a shame. It's such a beautiful state. I honestly can't imagine living anywhere else."

FOR BROOKE'S CALIFORNIA family and friends, the wedding in Paradise Valley, was a destination wedding, and while she'd worried about them traveling so far for the ceremony and reception, she obviously hadn't needed to have been stressed, not by the distance or the weather, because while it snowed off and on during the photos, her guests tramped happily through the powdery stuff from the venue's parking lot to reach the big Emerson Barn. The guests' excited chatter only stopped once the musicians played the first note, and then all fell silent, turning to watch as the mother of the bride was escorted down the aisle.

Amanda remained with Brooke until it was time for the bride to walk down the aisle.

"I'm so nervous," Brooke confessed, taking her father's arm.

Her father just patted her hand, every bit as nervous as his daughter. Amanda gave her a smile as she straightened the train on Brooke's gown, and then fluffed the long veil. "You look magnificent," she whispered in Brooke's ear. "Now go enjoy yourself."

Amanda waited for Brooke to reach her groom before slipping into the seat Tyler had saved for her. He'd taken a seat in the last row which meant she wasn't disturbing anyone else.

Tyler smiled at her as she sat down. "Everything go okay?"

"She was nervous, but I think she's okay now," she whispered.

"Have you ever met a bride that wasn't nervous?"

"No."

It wasn't a long service because Scott didn't want an overly formal service, but when the sun peeked through clouds during the ceremony, illuminating the bride and groom as they said their vows, Amanda got goose bumps. It was an absolutely beautiful moment, sacred and sweet, and the golden light shone through the big barn window, gilding Brooke and Scott, until the end of the ceremony when the minister proclaimed Brooke and Scott, man and wife.

"You can't get much more picture-perfect than that," Tyler said as the couple processioned out.

"No, you can't," she softly agreed.

They talked during dinner, and talked as they sipped champagne, and toasted the bride and groom, and then talked after the cake had been cut. They talked about their families, and the things that they'd learned in life, as well as the things that disappointed them.

"What matters most to you?" he asked, as the waiter passed out the squares of wedding cake.

"Besides, this delicious cake?" she teased.

"Which do you like better? Frosting or cake?"

"Both. I like them together." She smiled at him. "Honesty matters to me. I value honesty, integrity, and the ability to live within one's means." She saw his expression and she shrugged. "The opposite of catastrophe. I'm not a fan of catastrophe."

"But you seem to enjoy chaos."

"How so?"

"Aren't you a bit of a rebel?"

"Actually, I'm not." And then she understood that he was referencing her pink house. "You mean, because I painted my salon pink? I did that just because it was fun. It made me laugh. I was sure that after the shock wore off, you'd laugh, too."

"I did."

Amanda grinned. "But it's been a good business decision, too." She reached for her phone and typed in a link and showed him the article. "See? That pink paint job? The very thing you mocked? It's gotten me thousands of dollars of free publicity. The salon has been in the paper, and on the evening news."

He read the article, only looking up at her when he'd finished. "This article is not flattering. They said your house is tawdry and demeaning, reminiscent of a cheap paperback romance."

"Exactly."

"And you like that?"

"I can't buy this publicity. The phone is ringing off the hook with new bookings. If this continues, we're going to finally be able to expand our services, adding a masseuse and an aesthetician. By summer we'll be Marietta's only true day spa and salon."

"That is impressive," he agreed.

"Now I just need to get the mobile salon up and running and I'll be ready to take over the world."

He raised his champagne flute. "To a pink universe."

She laughed and they clinked rims and then Amanda didn't know how it happened, but the flutes were down on the table and he was pulling her toward him and kissing her, his hand in her hair, his mouth slanting over hers, making her feel a thousand wonderful things. He wasn't just smart, with a gorgeous face. Tyler Justice could kiss. And she didn't know if it was the champagne bubbles or Tyler's influence, but she didn't care that it was a public kiss, and that all of the wedding guests could see. She just wanted the kiss to go on and, oh, it did, hot, provocative, as well as maddeningly sweet. She lightly brushed his jaw with the bristle of a beard and loved how warm he felt, and wanted to be even closer than this.

"Talk about something," he growled, breaking the kiss off. "Distract me. Otherwise I'll kiss you again."

"Is that a bad thing?"

"Only if stories get back to Gram."

"And knowing Bette, she'll jump ahead and start making assumptions and plans for the future."

"You think?"

"Absolutely. Another kiss like that and she'll be telling people we're engaged and planning a June wedding."

He laughed and rose, extending his hand to her. "Dance with me."

Tyler led her onto the edge of the dance floor, not far from the huge arched window, which had been the backdrop for the ceremony earlier. There was no one in that particular spot, nearly everyone else choosing the middle of the dance floor, where it was brightly lit. It was a slow song and Tyler pulled her close, and she moved into his arms as if it was the most natural thing in the world. And maybe it was, she thought, as he held her securely, his body hard and warm, strange and yet also familiar. They danced in the shadows, and it felt as if they had the entire barn to themselves, even though it was just a few feet, while outside the big arched window, huge white snowflakes slowly tumbled from the sky.

It had been a long time since she'd danced, and even longer since she'd danced with someone that made her feel like this. He was so warm, and he smelled delicious. It was all she could do to keep from nuzzling his chest, or trying to get closer to his neck, and when their steps slowed even more, so they were barely moving on the edge of the dance floor where the light was dim, and shadows crept across the old planks of the barn floor.

This, she thought, gazing out the window at the glorious world of white where the only movement was the fall of lazy, lacey snowflakes, had to be the most romantic date she'd ever had, and it wasn't even supposed to be a date. It'd just happened.

And it just happened to be perfect.

CHAPTER EIGHT

M ONDAY MORNING TYLER woke up eager for his call with Cormac Sheenan despite having spent the night tossing and turning, playing the call out in his head, trying to imagine all the different outcomes, even while cautioning himself to remain calm and cordial no matter what Cormac said.

Cormac had all the power right now and Tyler just hoped Cormac would hear him out, because there were things Tyler hadn't done yet, games he hadn't created, ideas he hadn't shared. If Cormac was interested in doing something new, and developing innovative games and software, Tyler could help him get there.

After half a cup of Gram's tragically weak black coffee, he headed out for a run, his path taking him past the little pink house on Church Street. It was impossible for him to go anywhere without passing Amanda's place. Her lights were on upstairs. He wondered if she was out for a run now. Just thinking about her, and the possibility of seeing her, made him run a little faster, adrenaline pumping.

He hadn't seen her since Saturday night. It had only

been a day and yet he missed her. He wasn't used to missing people. He wasn't accustomed to this impatient desire… the missing rather like an ache in his chest.

He loved kissing her. She had incredible lips. She had incredible eyes. When she smiled her entire face lit up, and that smile and the light in her eyes did something to him. It made him feel protective, as well as strangely possessive, and he wasn't a possessive person. But every time he saw Amanda something inside of him wanted to claim her, and, yes, it was unreasonable because he hadn't known her all that long, but she felt like his, and the little voice inside him whispered *mine, mine, mine.*

But she wasn't his, at least not yet. And it was unlikely she'd want to be his if he acted like a caveman around her. Amanda was a gorgeous, smart, funny, kind woman, but also a very independent woman, and he was going to have to figure out a way to win her heart while keeping all the other males in Marietta away.

AMANDA WAS APPROACHING the courthouse on her return from River Bend Park, footsteps crunching the packed snow on the trail, when she spotted Tyler heading toward her.

She knew the moment he recognized her, because his expression changed, his hard, square jaw easing, his lips lifting in a crooked smile.

That crooked twist of his lips tugged on her heart, and

suddenly she felt breathless when moments ago she was fine. And yet, she was so glad to see him. She'd half-hoped she'd bump into him on her run, and now here he was.

"Hey," she said slowing as she approached him, her breath clouding on the cold morning air.

He stopped, too, and they faced each other in the middle of Crawford Park, each smiling a rather goofy smile for so early in the morning. "How was it?" he asked.

"Lots of ice. Probably not the best day to be running."

"But you did it anyway."

"It was that or run stairs at the high school stadium, and those can be icy as well, so I figured I'd stick with the river trail."

"In winter, wouldn't running on a treadmill be safer?"

"Maybe, but it'd also be boring. I've never been a fan of hot, sweaty gyms."

"I think you're thinking of saunas," he deadpanned.

Amanda laughed out loud, and he grinned, pleased by her response. "That was good," she admitted.

His grin widened, even more pleased. "What are you doing later?"

"Working."

"After work."

"Not much."

"Come over tonight. I'll make dinner."

"At your grandmother's?"

"She has a kitchen."

"Ha-ha." She adjusted her cap. "But seriously, what will she think if I come over?"

"She'll think I enjoy spending time with you." His gaze met hers and held. "And I do."

Amanda's pulse quickened, her heart skipping a beat. "Bette takes these things seriously," she said, fighting to sound normal. "She'll think it's going somewhere."

"Maybe it is."

She felt her eyes widen and her heart did that crazy leap thing again. He was smiling at her, and yet the expression in his eyes was surprisingly earnest.

She didn't know whether she should giggle, blush, or lean in to kiss him. She clapped her gloved hands together. "Don't you have that call today with Cormac?"

"I do. And why are you changing the subject?"

This time she couldn't hide the heat rushing through her, warming her face. "Because I'm not sure what to say."

"Say yes you'll come to dinner. I'll make my famous lasagna and garlic bread. You'll love it. And if you don't love it now, you will because it's one of the few things I know how to make."

"You're making all kinds of assumptions, handsome."

It was his turn to slowly smile, his straight white teeth flashing. "Am I?"

She shook her head and began jogging in place. "I'm getting cold. I have to go. And, yes, you're handsome. I'm sure you know it."

"It never hurts to hear."

She groaned even as she laughed. "Look who's become the funny man."

"You make me happy."

Her feet slowed. She stopped jogging. "Do I?" she asked softly, all laughter gone.

He nodded, and leaning forward, kissed her. "Yes." He kissed her again, then tugged her cap lower, all the way down her brow. "Go home and get warm. And I'll tell Gram you're coming for dinner."

AMANDA HAD BEEN to Bette's house countless times, and knew her way around the house and kitchen, and yet it was suddenly completely different being there with Tyler. He made the rooms feel small, and overly warm, and she kept bumping into walls and corners of furniture—the couch, the sideboard, the dining room table. She didn't feel any pain from the bumps, just klutzy. And giddy. And overly excited.

Tyler's lasagna was good, very respectable, and while it was in no way the best she'd ever had, his garlic bread probably was. The outside was lovely and crusty while the inside melted in her mouth, all warm soft bread fragrant with garlic and real butter. She ate two slices, and then another, mopping up the red sauce from the lasagna, while silently telling herself she'd just have to run an extra fifteen minutes but it would be worth it.

After dinner, Bette settled in to her reclining armchair to watch her favorite show and Tyler took a seat on the couch, and then patted the cushion next to him, indicating that Amanda was to sit next to him. Amanda darted a look in Bette's direction and Bette said loudly, "I know all about you two. Just ignore me. Pretend I'm not here."

Tyler shrugged. "She said to ignore her."

"As if," Amanda muttered, taking the empty spot next to him, and then privately delighted when he slid an arm around her and pulled her even closer.

"Feel like you're back in high school?" he asked in her ear.

Amanda fought a giggle. "I do. And it's weird."

"And nice."

She couldn't stop smiling. She didn't even feel sixteen anymore, but closer to eleven. "So how did it go with Cormac today?"

"The call got postponed at the last minute," he answered.

"That must have been disappointing."

"A little," he said.

She glanced up into his face. He didn't seem worried. "Has it been rescheduled yet?"

"No."

"You're not anxious?"

"No. Because I'm going to stop by his office tomorrow to see him."

Amanda went to bed humming songs from show tunes.

She couldn't remember when she last felt so happy. If this was love, no wonder people found it so addictive. She suddenly stopped pulling the throw pillows off her bed, freezing in place.

If this was love?

No.

That was just ridiculous. She wasn't in love, or falling in love. She'd only met Tyler two weeks ago. She couldn't be in love. She was simply infatuated. She had a crush. He was handsome, and athletic, creative and successful... as well as Bette's only grandchild, and determined to move her away from Marietta.

Amanda climbed into bed, no longer humming. She pulled the covers up to her chin and held her breath, trying to ignore the hint of panic. She was nearing twenty-eight. She'd dated plenty of nice men, but she'd never once come close to falling in love, so why now? Why Tyler? What made him special?

Everything, answered the little voice inside of her.

TYLER CONTINUED TO have a difficult time connecting with Cormac Sheenan. Either Cormac was constantly out of the office, or he had an incredibly efficient front desk receptionist who was operating under instructions to let no one past her.

Instead of getting annoyed, Tyler poured his energy into

a new, secret project, as well as a new game he'd wanted to work on for quite some time, but TexTron hadn't been enthused about new games. They just wanted to capitalize on what had already been created. Well, he didn't have to answer to TexTron anymore. He didn't have to answer to anyone anymore, which meant he could devote hours every day to his project, as well as coding and designing, and all the things he'd once loved to do before running the business got in the way of creating.

Tyler wasn't the only one immersed in work. Time seemed to fly by for Amanda. Her days were spent at the salon, and her evenings were more often than not spent with Tyler. Some nights they stayed in Marietta, while other nights they headed to Bozeman or Livingston. Amanda enjoyed showing off the neighboring communities, but was always glad to return to Marietta. It was small, but it was home.

Except it wasn't his home, she knew, glancing at Tyler one night as he drove them home from Bozeman where they'd gone to watch the Montana State Bobcats play Eastern Washington. "When do you plan on returning to Austin?" she asked.

"I don't know," he answered. "There really is no reason to be there anymore."

She processed this for a moment. "What about your house?"

"I'll have to sell it."

"The house isn't ready to sell though, is it?"

"No."

She wanted to ask more questions. She wanted to ask if he had a time frame for putting the house on the market. She wanted to know if he was planning on eventually returning to California—it was where he was from, after all—or if he was going to stay in Montana longer. She didn't want to worry about the future, but she was finding it increasingly difficult to manage her feelings. She was becoming so attached, and Amanda was beginning to think of them as a couple. Was that a mistake? Was he just killing time with her, or did he have deeper feelings? It had been so long since she'd dated anyone seriously that she couldn't even remember how this worked. All she knew was that it felt right being together. She wasn't a different person with him, she was just a little happier, and a whole lot more content. But if he wasn't going to stay in Marietta long-term, maybe she needed to do a better job protecting her heart?

He must have picked up on her pensive mood, because he lifted her hand and brought it to his lips, kissing the back of her fingertips. "What's wrong?"

It was such a sweet gesture, and the fact that he could read her so well, put a lump in her throat. She'd really fallen for this guy, hadn't she? "Can you see yourself in Montana long-term?" she asked carefully, as he put her hand on the stick shift, his fingers laced through hers. "I know your father didn't have fond memories of Marietta, but what do you think of it? You've been here a couple weeks now. Is it a place you could live?"

He hesitated. "If I had work here, I could see trying it for a couple of years."

"But only a couple of years."

He hesitated again, even longer this time. She could tell he was choosing his words with care. Clearly, he did not want to offend her.

"I have never lived in a place that wasn't urban," he said. "I was born in the Bay Area, I thrived in the Bay Area, I like cities."

"The traffic doesn't bother you? The smog doesn't bother you? Having people constantly on top of you..."

"No." His shoulders shifted, his expression rueful. "I know cities aren't for everyone, but I find them energizing. I wake up ready to get to work, get things done."

"You don't think people in smaller towns feel the same way?"

"Good question. Maybe they do. But, in general, small towns have never been for me."

Amanda bit her tongue to keep from saying more, even as disappointment filled her. She should have expected this. He'd never once said anything about wanting to spend more time in Montana. He'd merely said he wanted his company back, and instead she'd created an elaborate daydream, picturing him settling down in Marietta, working at Cormac's headquarters on Main and Fourth Street, and the two of them figuring out their relationship. In her mind it was idyllic—him, her, working, happy and fulfilled. In Marietta. She realized now it was a mistake. She didn't even have to read romances to live in fantasyland.

He shot her a side glance. "You've gone awfully quiet."

"Just thinking."

"About?"

"How different we are." She forced a small, tight smile. "You don't like small towns. I don't like big cities—"

"I said *in general* I didn't like small towns. I didn't say I didn't like Marietta. In case you haven't noticed, I'm enjoying my visit."

Visit. Visit as in visitor. He wasn't staying.

"I'm enjoying it so much that I just bought tickets this morning for us to go to the St. Patrick's Day Ball at the Graff Hotel Saturday night. I know Gram was wanting to go, and I thought I'd check with you and see how you felt if she went with us?"

Amanda didn't know how to answer. Her emotions were all over the place. She'd never been to any of the balls or parties at the Graff. The ticket prices were usually too steep and she didn't have a significant other to take her. Instead, she did the hair for all those going, and suddenly she felt a little bit like Cinderella being invited to the ball herself. "Of course I would want you to take Bette," she answered huskily. "She's far more deserving than me."

"But dancing with her isn't the same as dancing with

you," he teased.

She felt the corners of her lips lift. He made her smile even when she didn't want to. "Does she know yet?"

"I wanted to get your approval first."

"You never have to do that. She's your grandmother."

He gave her hand a squeeze as he shifted down, slowing to brake at the stop light on Highway 89 near the new development on the edge of Marietta. "But you're my girl."

Her heart skipped a beat and she turned to look at him, her gaze locking with his. Even in the shadowy light of the car, she could see the intensity in his expression. "Am I?" she said, trying to sound light and flirtatious, but instead the words came out a little too rough, and raw. Maybe it was because she cared so much about his answer.

"I'm not interested in anyone but you, Amanda."

"We had a rocky start."

"It wasn't that rocky."

"No?"

"No. I pretty much fell for you the moment I laid eyes on you."

THE BALL AT the Graff was equal parts fun and fabulous, but maybe that was because Tyler looked dashing in his dark suit and tie, while Amanda felt like a princess in her gorgeous vintage 1950s ball gown, light gold fabric shimmering in the light, the full skirt swirling around her legs reminding her of the short-lived months she'd been able to take ballet before her mother pulled her out due to financial difficulties. But she felt like a ballerina tonight, with just a little Hollywood film star thrown in for glamour. By Marietta standards she was overdressed. But then, by Marietta standards she was always overdressed, and it didn't bother her because she enjoyed dressing up, and this was home, and if she couldn't be herself here, then where?

The Graff ballroom was awash in green, with shamrock garland swags over each of the ballroom windows and more garlands over each of the ballroom doors. The tables, too, were dressed in green, with festive emerald fabric topping the white fabric below. The centerpieces of white roses, carnations and shamrocks were so charming that Amanda suspected Risa had designed them, and she paused near a table to admire how the glowing votive candles reflected the shamrocks' green glitter.

"Ah, this is lovely," Amanda said, her gaze sweeping the room. "I'm so happy to be here. I've always wanted to come to one of these fundraisers."

"I tried to bring you," Bette said. "But you didn't want to be my date."

"I didn't want to be a pity date," Amanda corrected with a quick smile.

"No pity dates here tonight," Tyler added. "Not when I have the two most beautiful women in the ballroom on my arms."

While servers made the rounds with festive cocktails and green beer, Amanda pointed out various people to Tyler that she thought he should know, or might recognize the name, such as Sage Carrigan O'Dell, who'd founded Copper Mountain Chocolates, Paul and Bailey Zabrinski, owners of Big Z Hardware and Lumber on Main Street, and then Risa and her gorgeous husband, Monty, with Amanda adding that she was sure Risa had done the flowers for the party tonight. "Risa is involved in every charity event here in town. She's so quick to donate time and materials. Whenever I need anything for a special event donation, she always says yes."

"Sounds like a wonderful person," Tyler answered.

"Oh! And there's Rachel Vaughn, her husband Nate is co-owner of the Bar V5 Dude Ranch. We have a number of successful dude ranches in the area, but the Bar V5 is one of the most successful. You might have seen Rachel's bakery on Main Street. Copper Mountain Gingerbread and Dessert Factory? That's my go-to place for birthday cakes. I love their cakes."

"But Main Street Diner for pies," Bette interjected, tapping Tyler on the arm. "That's where I got your apple pie."

Amanda nodded. "I agree. Ownership of the diner has changed several times over the years, but they have the same cook in the back, and she comes in at four every morning to get the baking started."

"You can tell the cowboys in the room, can't you?" Tyler

said, nodding at the crowded ballroom where Marietta's finest mingled, voices a hum of conversation and laughter, guests wearing everything from suits and tuxes and formal gowns to crisp plaid shirts and starched, ironed Wranglers.

"Not necessarily. Our mayor loves to dress up in Western gear, and wear his most expensive boots, but he lives on Bramble and wouldn't know a heifer from a steer."

Amanda then gestured toward a group of men in tuxedos with glamorous wives, women Amanda knew quite well as she did the hair for all. She'd started with McKenna years ago, and then McKenna Douglas Sheenan recommended her to Harley, Taylor, Whitney, with the most recent being Jet, Harley's youngest sister and the wife of Shane, the brother the town called 'the lost Sheenan.' "And those fellows over there, they were all raised in Paradise Valley, and could probably ride before they could walk. Those are the Sheenans." She gave Tyler a faint smile. "Cormac is the fair one in the middle, his wife Whitney works at Sheenan Media as well. The rest of the Sheenan brothers are dark. Only four of the six are here tonight. Brock, the oldest, is the one on the far left, then Cormac, Troy and Trey." She held Tyler's gaze. "Want me to introduce you to them?"

"No."

"Not even Cormac?"

"I might approach him, but I can handle it on my own."

"I'm not saying you need me."

"I know. But I just have to do this my way." He turned

to his grandmother. "How are you doing, Gram? Still good standing, or would you like to sit down?"

"I'm ready to sit," Bette said.

"Let's find our table."

Reaching their table, Bette was delighted to discover that it was filled with her closest friends from her bridge club and birthday group. She went around to each of the ladies, exclaiming over their dresses, admiring fun shamrock rhinestone pins and earrings. She hugged and kissed them all, and Amanda grinned, happy to see Bette so radiant. Amanda truly felt as if her night had been made.

"Did you do this?" she asked Tyler, glancing up at him.

"I thought she'd get a kick out of being with her friends."

"She's having the time of her life."

"I'm glad. She deserves to be spoiled. I should have been doing these things for her years ago."

"But you are now, and that's what matters. Now tell me, how did you pull it off?"

"I bought a table and then reached out to each of her friends on movie day."

"You went to the movies with everyone again?"

"Yeah. It's our thing."

Amanda laughed, and impulsively gave him a squeeze, feeling incredibly lucky, just like the Irish.

"You're beautiful," he said, quietly.

"It's the dress—"

"No, it's you. *You* are beautiful."

He'd paid her compliments before but tonight she felt the warmth and appreciation wrap her heart. She wanted this to work between them, she really did, and she thought it could, if he lived here. *If* being the key word. "Thank you," she murmured, eyes stinging, chest tender with emotion she wasn't prepared to analyze, not tonight, not here, not when she felt so much like Cinderella at the ball.

Tyler held out her chair and she was just about to sit down when a hard voice spoke behind them. "What did you do to that house, Amanda? You ruined it. Why would you paint it pink?"

Amanda tensed at the sound of the hard, bitter voice, not at all happy to hear it. It'd been months since she'd last seen Kirk. Why did she have to bump into him now, and here of all places?

"What's wrong with the pink exterior?" Tyler said, shocking her, because she knew Tyler wasn't a big fan of the pink, either.

"You must be the new boyfriend," Kirk answered, giving Tyler the once-over as he extended his hand. "Kirk Jackson, founder and president of Jackson Construction. And the old boyfriend."

It was on the tip of her tongue to say he'd never been her boyfriend, but before she could speak, Tyler did. "You don't look that old," he said jovially, taking Kirk's hand, and giving it a firm shake.

Kirk didn't smile. He let go of Tyler's hand as quickly as he could. "Didn't catch your name."

"Tyler Justice."

"Any relation to Don and Bette Justice?"

Tyler nodded toward Bette at the table. "Grandson."

"Didn't know Bette had family in town."

Tyler didn't answer, and Kirk shifted uncomfortably before shooting Amanda a narrowed glance. "You never called me back."

She frowned, perplexed. "When did you call?"

"Right around the holidays."

"If you called, I didn't get the message."

"I called, and I left a message."

Amanda told herself to ignore his tone. She told herself to ignore everything about him. He wasn't her problem. Yes, she'd gone out with him a couple times, but it was a mistake and a long time ago.

"Maybe you should talk to your receptionist," he added. "She promised to give you the message."

Her chin lifted. "I will speak to her. Enjoy your evening. Take care, Kirk." And then she moved to sit, and Tyler was holding her chair and Kirk had no choice but to move on.

After sitting down, Amanda and Tyler were quiet for a long moment.

Tyler broke the silence. "Interesting guy," he said, his tone casual, and yet she sensed he wasn't as disinterested as he appeared.

"Think so?" she replied, glancing up at him.

"He has a strong personality." He paused. "Especially when it comes to you."

"Unfortunately."

"Were you together a long time?"

"We went out a few times, a couple years ago. He wasn't for me, but he's had a hard time letting it go."

"You're kidding."

She shrugged. "I try to ignore him, but I confess, he makes my skin crawl."

"I came really close to punching him."

"I'm glad you didn't. I don't think your grandmother would approve."

"Oh, Gram would approve, especially if she knew how much he bothered you." Tyler turned his head to watch Kirk move through the room. "And now he's bothering me."

Amanda smothered a laugh. "No fighting allowed. This is a ball. It's supposed to be fun."

Tyler's attention was still on Kirk who was now waiting in line at one of the bars in the corner of the room. "Tell me about him."

"There's nothing to say. We went out a few times. He was loud, and opinionated, and I chose not to go out on with him again. He didn't like it. I admire confidence, but his is misplaced. He'd stop by my work uninvited and just kind of... be Kirk."

"And these dates were when?"

"Two years ago in May."

"And he's still a possessive jerk?"

She exhaled. "Is it that obvious?"

"Yes." Tyler's brow creased. He was clearly baffled by something. "What did you like about him? Why go out with him in the first place?"

She fidgeted in her seat. "Marietta is a small town. He was new. He'd moved to the area to build that new shopping area on the outside of town. He came in to the old salon I managed on Main Street for a haircut. He returned the next day and asked me out. I said yes."

"But he's a jerk."

"I didn't see it right away. And when you know everyone in town, it's kind of exciting to be asked out by someone new. I was hopeful, and flattered."

"Huh."

"You asked."

"I just can't believe you'd be flattered by the attention of someone like that—"

"You've grown up in cities where you don't know most of the people around you. Everyone is new, and interesting. The world is filled with possibilities. It's not the same for me. Most of the men in Marietta I've known since elementary school."

He drummed his fingers on the table. "Is that why you went out with me? Because I was the new guy in town?"

"No. And if you recall, I didn't want to go out with you.

If you recall, I was only being nice to you because I had to be, for Bette's sake." She arched a brow. "You weren't someone I wanted to like. And for your information, I still struggle with the fact that you are just visiting, and any day now, you could leave and not return." She met his gaze and held it. "True?"

"I don't know the future, no. But no one does."

"But most people know if they want to live one place or another. I know I want to live in Marietta. You can't say that, though."

Tyler didn't answer, thinking he hadn't seen any of this coming. One moment everything was wonderful, and she was smiling up at him, making him feel like he was on top of the world, and now everything was tense and strained.

"How did that Kirk guy hijack our night?" he asked, trying to make a joke of it, thinking they needed to turn things around, and quickly.

"I don't know if he did, or we have finally bumped against reality." She adjusted her tiny star earring, the star made of rhinestones. "It was bound to happen. We are so different—"

"What are you doing?"

"Just laying all the cards on the table. I think we should, don't you? Better do it now, before someone gets hurt."

He leaned toward her, his gaze locking with hers, challenging her. "I think you're running scared. I think you're afraid to fall for me, because you'd be vulnerable, and you'd be risking your heart."

"No one wants to be hurt."

"You're right. I don't want to be hurt. It's not at all appealing. But do you know what's even less appealing? Losing you. I'm not ready to let you go, Amanda, not when we're just beginning to figure this out, because I think we have something good here. I think we have something special. Don't you?"

He saw the different emotions cross her features, the hurt and fear, waging war with hope and tenderness, and in between the different emotions he saw her, and just how vulnerable she was. Amanda put on a good front, and she had a successful business, but underneath, she was far more fragile than he'd expected.

"I like you," she said finally, her voice pitched low.

"Good, because I really like you."

"I don't want to be hurt."

"I have no desire to hurt you."

"But you could very well leave tomorrow."

"Probably not tomorrow, but yes, I could leave. But if things worked between us, I could ask you to come with me. Go somewhere new. Have an adventure with me."

"I'd go on a vacation, but I don't want to move. This is my home. This is where I belong."

"You wouldn't move, even for love?" he asked.

She paled, and drew a shallow, shuddering breath. "That's not a fair question."

"Why not?"

"Because the reason I live here, is for love. I love my sister, Charity, dearly. I love my parents—even as difficult as they are. I love my friends like your grandmother. I belong here because they're here. We're not just a family, but a community."

He could see she was getting upset. Tears filmed her eyes and he leaned forward and pressed a kiss to her brow. "Don't cry."

"I'm not," she answered, blinking hard.

Maybe she wasn't crying, but she was definitely fighting tears, and watching her struggle to maintain control did something to him, making his chest tighten and ache. He was so used to her smiling and laughing, and he loved her laugh because it was warm and husky and impossibly happy, that her sadness wounded him, making him want to better protect her.

Amanda Wright was so much more than a beautiful face. She was smart and kind, generous, and optimistic, and he wanted more of her in his life, not less.

She was habit-forming. Charming, maddening, fascinating, intoxicating—

He liked her. Possibly loved her.

Probably loved her, as he couldn't remember when he last felt this way about anyone.

In just a matter of weeks, she'd become as—if not more—interesting than his work. Instead of focusing on games, he found himself thinking about her. Analyzing her. And every time he was sure that he finally figured her out, she surprised him, and showed a different side to her. She wasn't shallow. She wasn't vain. She wasn't self-absorbed. If anything, she was the exact opposite. She loved others and gave of herself unstintingly. She didn't wait for others to do the right thing. Amanda seemed to be the first to volunteer, and the last to leave.

Tyler had spent the past fifteen years designing bestselling games, games that reviewers called dangerously addictive, but Amanda was far more meaningful and engrossing than anything he'd ever created, and if she loved Marietta so much, could he come to love it the way she did? Could he possibly make it his home?

CHAPTER NINE

T HE MEETING WITH Cormac ended up happening very differently from how Tyler had imagined, coming about Tuesday as Tyler walked out of Java Café with a cup of coffee and Cormac was just heading in.

Tyler recognized Cormac right away, and was wondering if he should say something when Cormac stopped him. "Aren't you Tyler Justice?" Cormac asked.

"Yes," he answered, extending a hand. "You're Cormac."

"I owe you a couple phone calls and a meeting. I'm sorry. I've been on the road more than I've been home lately. My family isn't happy about it, and I'm just trying to get caught up with everything on the desk. You should know you're near the top of the list. I was going to give you a call today. Or do you have a few minutes right now?"

"I do."

"Let me get some coffee and then we'll sit down and talk." Cormac opened the door to Java Café, and Tyler followed him in.

Their conversation lasted far longer than either of them anticipated. Cormac told him a little bit about why he wanted to buy Justice Games, and then they discussed the industry, and how changing technology kept changing the way people played games, and not just where they played them, but how. They ended up speaking for close to two hours and when it was over Cormack asked bluntly, "So what do you want from me?"

"I want to continue my work," Tyler answered, just as direct. "I want to remain with Justice Games, and while I understand I no longer own the company, I don't see why I couldn't remain involved in some capacity. Either as a lead designer or as a creative director."

"Why did you sell to TexTron in the first place?"

"Because it's awfully hard to build a company, and continually design new games, and I realized I couldn't do justice to both—" He paused, cracked a smile. "No pun intended. I realized over time that my passion is for design. I'm a nerd. I'm happiest when coding and doing my graphics, not crunching numbers or worrying about market share or market dominance."

"Was it difficult for you, working for TexTron?"

"The only time it was truly difficult was when they sold to you. I had no idea it was coming, and I was caught off guard. I felt powerless and I didn't like it. I still don't."

"But if you worked for me, you'd still be powerless. I could decide to offload Justice Games tomorrow."

"You could, absolutely. But you might also end up keeping the company, realizing it's exciting and rewarding and twenty years from now we could be sitting here again, congratulating ourselves for making it even more successful."

"What do you want financially?"

"What I had with TexTron. A base salary and then a percentage of profits."

"Your base salary wasn't significant."

"But the potential is there if the company is run right."

"You didn't earn significantly while you were in Austin."

"Justice Games wasn't properly managed, no."

"Why don't I just give you a bigger salary?"

"Because my compensation should be tied to the success of my games. I've always said that, and I still believe it."

Cormac studied him for a long minute. "When would you want to start?"

"Tomorrow."

For the first time since they sat down, his firm mouth eased and Cormac smiled. "How about Monday? We're still sorting out relocation details and trying to find adequate office space."

"I can tell you what we need."

"I'm sure you could." Cormac's smile broadened. "By the way, I hear you ride." He must have seen Tyler's confusion because he added, "Mandy told me you snowboard."

"I haven't for a couple of years. Texas isn't known for its slopes."

"No vacations for you?"

"I have a hard time unplugging. Something I know I

need to work on." Tyler hesitated. "When did you see Mandy?"

"Saturday. She cut my hair the day of the St. Patrick's Day Ball. I told her to introduce us at the hotel, but I guess it didn't work out."

Tyler remembered how Amanda had offered to introduce him to Cormac at the ball, and how he'd rejected the offer because he'd wanted to handle it himself. "She's pretty amazing."

"She's been through a lot. Take care of her."

Tyler left Java Café feeling better than he had in weeks.

He'd be working again come Monday. He was enjoying being in Marietta. And then there was Amanda.

She was incredible, and she made him wonder if they could go the distance. Life was so much better with her in it. And while he'd never found the idea of marriage particularly appealing, not after his parents' marriage had fallen apart, Amanda made him want to try.

He needed to talk to her. There were things they needed to discuss. Even before today's conversation with Cormac, Tyler had been thinking of remaining in Marietta. He'd even poured over the *Copper Mountain Courier* classified ads, looking to see what was available in terms of office space.

Settling down in Marietta was a new idea, something that had only come to him recently, and it was still so fresh that he wasn't sure what to think of it, and he didn't want to say anything to Amanda until he knew for certain it wasn't an impulsive decision.

But something she'd said to him a couple weeks ago had stayed with him.

Why did his grandmother have to leave all of her friends? Why should she be the one to move? Why couldn't he move here?

There was no reason for him to live in Texas now. He'd never truly settled in, and even though he had a house in Austin, it wasn't home. California was home. Or once upon a time it had been home. But he'd cut a lot of ties when he'd moved to Texas, and he'd let a lot of relationships go. He didn't feel any burning desire to return to California for that matter.

He could buy a big house in Marietta and have Gram move in with him. Or, he could stay with Gram in her house until they figured out what the right thing to do was, because the more time he spent with his grandmother, the more he'd come to appreciate her independence and spirit, as well as her dozens of friends.

He imagined trying to tell Gram that he had decided to move to Marietta. The first thing she'd ask is why, and he'd be honest with her. It was Amanda. She'd changed him. And with all her projects and dreams, she seemed to be changing Marietta, too.

"COME FOR DINNER tonight," Bette said Tuesday afternoon,

as she dropped into her pink chair at the salon, the one reserved just for her. "I'm making chicken something," she added before looking at her reflection and lifting a curl, trying to give it a little height.

Amanda checked her smile. Most of Amanda's clients were used to Bette coming and going. "Eileen, you know Bette Justice, don't you?" she said, introducing her client in her chair to Bette.

Eileen gave a small nod, unable to do more with Amanda adding silver highlights to her salt-and-pepper bob. "Oh yes, our sons grew up together, and played football and baseball at Marietta High." Eileen's eyebrows arched as she tried to look toward Bette. "I heard your grandson is back, isn't he?"

"Tyler, Patrick's son, yes." Bette stopped fussing with the curl and folded her hands in her lap. "I haven't seen you since you filled in for the duplicate bridge club. Are you still playing?"

"Not as much as I used to. Howard hasn't been well."

"I'm sorry to hear that."

"I suppose it's inevitable at our age, isn't it?"

"Yes, but it doesn't make it any easier."

For a moment there was silence, and a poignant resignation to the inevitability of life. Amanda swallowed around the lump filling her throat. So many of her clients were older women and she loved them fiercely because they had been through so much, and were so impossibly resilient. She didn't know how they did it. She wasn't sure she could ever be that strong.

"What time should I be there?" Amanda asked Bette, breaking the silence.

"What time do you finish today?"

"My last client is at five today, and it's just a cut and style, so I should be free by six if I let Emily close."

"Let Emily close for you and come to the house. I'll plan on serving dinner for six thirty. Tyler's a man, and men like to eat early."

Amanda choked on smothered laughter. "Did he say that?"

"No, but I know. Men get so grumpy if they don't eat at a decent hour." And then Bette was saying her goodbyes and bustling out.

"She hasn't changed a bit," Eileen said, as the salon door closed behind Bette. "Always cheerful, always taking care of others."

"You've known her a long time."

"Oh, at least fifty years. Her son, Patrick, and my boys grew up together. They met in elementary school and then went onto middle school and high school together, although back then, the middle school and high school were all part of the same building. She never had an easy time of it, though. Her husband was hard on her and their son. Everyone knew it. He was quite the disciplinarian, but what do you expect? He was former military, a retired lieutenant colonel, and he ran the house as if he was still in the army. I used to complain about Howard being bossy but Howard was a pussy cat compared to Don, and Howard had his faults, but he would never have tried to dictate to our children who they could date."

"Don did that?"

"It was Don's way or the highway."

"That's why Patrick left," Amanda said.

Eileen nodded. "And never returned."

DINNER AT BETTE'S had become a weekly tradition, and Tyler usually opened a bottle of good wine, but tonight instead of wine, champagne was chilling on ice.

"Champagne?" Amanda said, surprised to see the silver ice bucket on the dining room table, along with the trio of flutes. "What's happened? What are we celebrating?"

"Lots of things," he said, popping the cork, and filling the flutes.

He handed her a glass and he carried two into the kitchen where Bette was bustling around, and humming brightly, reminding Amanda of Snow White.

"I have some news," he said, giving his grandmother a flute, and then facing both. "On Monday, I report to Sheenan Media, although I'm not entirely sure where I'm actually working, but I met with Cormac today, and he's bringing me on."

"That is fantastic news," Bette cried.

"Champagne worthy indeed," Amanda added, smiling, clinking glasses with him and then his grandmother. "Why didn't you call me earlier, and tell me?"

"Because I wanted to be with you when I told you, and I wanted to thank you for always looking out for me, even when I don't know you are." He wrapped his arm around her waist and pulled her close. "I didn't realize you were supposed to introduce me to Cormac at the St. Patrick's Day Ball."

"I tried."

"I know you did."

"But honestly, I'm glad you didn't let me. It's better this way. It's all you."

They smiled at each other for a moment. "Does this mean you might be staying awhile?" Amanda asked softly.

"It means I'm going to look for a house."

Bette straightened from peeking into the oven, quilted orange hot mitts on her hands. "What? You're leaving me already?"

"I'm going to try to find something in the neighborhood. That way I can walk over for lunch and dinner and dessert."

"Not lunch," she protested. "I don't like fixing lunch. But dinner, and dessert, definitely. And speaking of dinner, I can't get anything done with you two underfoot. Take your bubbly and go into the living room. I've put some yearbooks on the coffee table. I thought you two would get a kick out of seeing your parents when they were back in high school."

Tyler and Amanda looked at each other.

Tyler lifted a brow.

"Our parents?" Amanda said, clarifying Bette's comment.

"Yes, your parents. They were just a year apart. Tyler's dad, Patrick, was a year older than your mom, Mandy."

"How do you remember that?" Amanda asked.

"I only had one child," she answered, turning back to the stove to stir something in a saucepan. "Look them up in the index and you'll be able to find them quickly."

As Tyler and Amanda headed to the living room, Tyler grabbed the bottle of champagne and topped off their glasses.

"They must have known each other then," Amanda said, sitting down on the living room couch and setting her flute on the coffee table so she could reach for the yearbook in front of her. "It's not a big high school."

Tyler sat down next to Amanda, and for the next few minutes, they went from the index to a photo, and then the index, to another, and it wasn't long before it became apparent that Patrick Justice and Julie Scranton didn't just know each other, they were *dating* each other. Amanda poured over the yearbooks and the photos and the captions and she discovered that it was a relationship that spanned years.

TYLER WAS SHOCKED.

He couldn't stop staring at the photo of his dad sitting

on a picnic table next to a beautiful blonde girl that looked almost exactly like Amanda. His arm was behind her and she was smiling up at his dad with clear affection. They were a striking couple, both handsome. His dad was the confident one though. Amanda's mom looked sweet, but rather shy.

Tyler glanced at Amanda and discovered she had tears in her eyes. "What's wrong?"

"I've never seen her look like this. I've never known her like this. She's so young here, and so pretty."

"My dad was a senior, and she was a junior, which meant she was what? Sixteen or seventeen?"

Amanda nodded. "They *dated*."

"For years."

"I had no idea she'd ever dated anyone but my dad." She blinked and tears fell. Amanda reached up and dashed them away.

"I knew your mom then." It was Bette in the doorway, her frilly apron tied over her dress, a spatula in her hand. "Used to have her over to the house all the time."

"Here? To this house?"

Bette nodded. "She was every bit as sweet as she looked. I liked her enormously. And I know she cared about me. She said I was like a mom to her."

"I don't understand," Tyler said. "Any of this."

"Neither do I," Amanda added unsteadily.

Bette sighed. "It's a long story, but there's a short version, I suppose."

"Thank you," Tyler muttered.

"Your dad, Tyler, fell in love with Mandy's mom almost right away."

"Let me guess, he was the quarterback and she was a cheerleader."

"Almost. He was the quarterback, but she wasn't a cheerleader. She couldn't afford the fees. Her family didn't have a lot of money."

Tyler heard Amanda's soft, sharp inhale and he reached for her hand, his fingers lacing with hers.

"They were very sweet together, your dad and Julie, but your grandfather didn't approve of the relationship. He didn't—admire—Julie's family, troubled by her family's history here in the valley, and he worried Julie would deliberately get pregnant, trapping your dad into marriage, so he put an end to the relationship." She shot Amanda a troubled glance before looking at Tyler. "It's what drove your dad from Montana, and it's why he never introduced Wendy, your mom, to him. Not until the day of the wedding."

"And Amanda's mom?" Tyler said gruffly. "What happened to her?"

"She met my dad," Amanda answered in a small voice. "And had three daughters with him."

For a moment there was just silence, and then Bette stirred. "I need to check my chicken," she said, turning around and returning to the kitchen.

Again, there was silence. Tyler didn't know what to say. The room felt thick with emotion, and he could feel Amanda's hand tremble in his. He tightened his fingers, pressing his palm to hers, holding her hand more closely.

"What are you thinking?" he asked after a long moment.

She just shook her head, the tears still there in her eyes, making them shine. "The more things change, the more they stay the same."

"What does that mean?"

"It means when you're poor, people assume the worst of you." Her head lifted, and her bright, fierce gaze met his. "It means you have no right to be pretty or smart, and if you work hard, it's a fluke because, God help you, you're little more than a gold digger or a social climber. Being poor shouldn't be a disease. It shouldn't be the stigma it is, either. I know why Jenny moved to Chicago after she left school. She wanted to escape Marietta and everyone who thought they knew her. I wish I'd moved, too." She wiped a hand across her eyes. "I wish I'd gone—"

He kissed her then, kissing her to silence the stream of words, kissing to try to distract her from the pain. He hated it when she hurt, and he most of all hated it when he, or his family, was responsible for that pain.

Her mouth quivered beneath his and her soft warm lips tasted of salt. Normally she kissed him back, but tonight she was too sad.

"I'm sorry," he murmured against her mouth before lifting his head and stroking a silky blonde tendril back from her cheek.

"Sorry you kissed me?" she said huskily, her cheeks flushed, her lips soft and pink and so very kissable.

"Sorry my grandfather was such an ass, and sorry society sucks—"

"It's alright. I'm stronger than I look."

"You've had a lot of adversity."

"And I'm successful because of it." She smiled a lopsided smile, but he was worried because the smile didn't reach her eyes.

THEY SOMEHOW MANAGED to get through dinner, although afterward Amanda couldn't remember what they discussed, or even what she ate. She sat at the table, feeling as if in a fog, her head cloudy, thoughts and emotions jumbling together.

It wasn't until Tyler cleared the plates, leaving Bette and Amanda alone together at the table, that Amanda asked, "All this time you've known I was Julie Scranton's daughter?"

"Yes," Bette answered.

Amanda didn't know where to look. She didn't know what to feel. "I don't understand," she said huskily.

She'd known Bette for years… almost half her life. Why keep this a secret?

Tyler entered the dining room with the cake and stopped

when he heard what they were discussing. "Why don't you two talk while I serve the cake?" Tyler suggested.

"I think I'll have to pass," Amanda said breathlessly, rising. "It's getting late and I'm fading quickly. But dinner was delicious, Bette. Thank you for including me again tonight."

Bette rose, too. "Don't leave yet! Let's have the rum cake first."

Amanda glanced at her watch. "Save me a piece, okay? Because you do make the best rum cake in all of Marietta, but I'm hosting a staff meeting before we open in the morning and I still have to prep for the meeting and then I should try to sleep—"

"But you're not going to be able to sleep, not either of you, if you don't talk now," Tyler interrupted. "I know you're upset, and so does Gram. Give her a chance to explain, Mandy. Please?"

Amanda stiffened. He'd just called her Mandy. Until now it had always been Amanda. She held her breath, air bottling in her lungs, until she felt a little dizzy, which only added to her confusion.

Tonight so many things had happened, and it was, frankly, too much. Small towns had tight connections, but this was a little too tight. Tyler's dad, Patrick, had dated her mom, and her mom, as a teenager, had spent hours in this very house.

Her mom had never said a word about the Justice family, or Bette, even though she knew Bette was her favorite client, and a dear friend.

And Bette… Bette had never said a word about knowing her mother, either.

The connections weren't just tight at the moment, they felt suffocating.

Amanda stood frozen in place, ambivalent and exhausted. She didn't know what to do. Her brain told her she should go home because she was too tired and sensitive to process anymore tonight and yet another part of her felt troubled and conflicted and didn't want to leave until things were resolved.

He left the dining room and she slowly sat back down. "Bette, this seems like a bad joke," she said after a moment.

And when the older woman said nothing, Amanda continued, "Why didn't you ever tell me that the girl Patrick was dating in high school, the one his father disapproved of, was my mother? Don't you think that was relevant to the story?"

"I wanted to, but then I also wanted to protect you. If you had never met Tyler, would it have mattered to you? Would it have changed things between us?"

"All I know is that I did meet Tyler, and it *has* changed things between us—"

"Please don't say that."

Amanda looked away, holding her breath, air bottled in her lungs, making her already aching chest burn. She held her breath so long that little spots danced before her eyes. She finally let the breath go, but when she exhaled, tears started to sting her eyes. She felt absolutely broken for reasons she couldn't even articulate. "Have you always known I was Julie's daughter?"

"Yes. You and your sisters look just like her, except her hair was a little darker blonde."

"Dad was the towhead," she said numbly.

Bette nodded. "He was very handsome. He caused quite a stir in town when he arrived."

"You remember all that?"

"I do."

"And you never thought to tell me any of this?"

"In all fairness, I thought it was Patrick's story to tell, not mine."

"Why? My mom doesn't matter? She's not allowed to have a voice?"

"Well, why didn't she tell you about Patrick? Why didn't she tell you about me? Have you never talked about me? Has she ever been to your salon and seen the chair with my name on it?"

"She has," Amanda answered in a low voice.

"But she didn't comment on it? She didn't ask questions?"

"No."

Bette said nothing, and Amanda was on her feet again, pacing the length of the dining room. She felt chilled and she rubbed her arms, trying to warm herself and yet the block of ice in her chest just seemed to grow larger, and colder. "I don't understand any of this." Her words came out broken. "I wish I didn't know any of this."

"It's why I never told you—"

"But why did you come to me in the first place? You were Nell's customer for thirty-five years. You were so loyal to her, and then I started there, and you switched to me and I never questioned it. I realize now I should have, but I was nineteen, just a college sophomore. It didn't cross my mind that there was any connection between us, other than you thought I was a talented stylist."

"You were, and are."

"But that's not why you switched from Nell, was it? You switched because I was Julie's daughter."

"I wanted to get to know you better, yes."

"Why didn't you just tell me then that you'd known my mother? Why never mention her all these years?"

"I cared about your mom. I had grown very close to her during those years she dated Patrick. When it all fell apart, I took it very hard. I missed her. I missed having her in my life. I missed having a girl in the house. Julie had become like a daughter to me—"

"*Please.* Please don't say that."

"Why? It's the truth."

"I don't know, but it's uncomfortable. And upsetting. Because if she was like a daughter to you, wouldn't you have had a relationship with her? If she was like a daughter, why don't you and she speak?"

"It's complicated."

"Or did your husband put his foot down, and you just fell in line? You and Patrick?"

"Patrick loved her."

"Right. Everybody loved her." Amanda could barely see through the tears. She was close to losing it, but she wouldn't do that here. She couldn't fall apart here, not in Bette's house. "I have to go. I can't listen to any more tonight. It's too much. Please tell Tyler goodbye."

TYLER WAS GLAD to have time alone in the kitchen while Gram and Amanda talked in the other room.

He hadn't allowed himself to dwell on his grandmother's revelations during dinner, but now that he had some time to himself, he was shocked by what he'd learned. His dad and Amanda's mom had dated in high school, and not just dated, but by all accounts, had been deeply in love. They'd been nearly inseparable for two and a half years. But then his grandfather had objected to Patrick's attachment to Julie, and so his dad left Montana, going to California for college to escape his father and his control. It explained plenty of things about the past, but not all.

Tyler stopped wiping down clean counters to listen as the living room had gone ominously quiet. He couldn't hear anything anymore. Dropping the dish towel he headed to the living room and found his grandmother still sitting at the dining room table, face covered, crying into her hands.

"Gram," he said, crouching next to her. "Sssh, don't cry. It's okay."

"It's not," she choked. "It might not ever be."

"Nonsense. Where did she go?"

"Home."

He lifted his head and looked to the door, surprised, and then not, that Amanda had left without saying goodbye. "It'll be fine. It will sort out soon."

"You didn't see the way she looked at me. She looked at me as if she didn't even know me... the same way Julie looked at me all those years ago after she and Patrick broke up. One day she was the daughter I'd never had, and the next, she was a stranger."

"Amanda's not going to cut you off. I promise you that."

"She's so hurt, Tyler. She's so hurt and it's all my fault."

CHAPTER TEN

TYLER FOLLOWED AMANDA home. She should have expected that. Instead she'd opened her door to him and now he was in her upstairs apartment, talking to her, trying to calm her down but every word he said only made her more upset because he didn't get it, he didn't understand Marietta, or the shame that had shadowed her every day of her life.

Her mother's family, the Scrantons, had been the poor white trash in Marietta. They didn't own a house, or land. They lived in a trailer way back behind the railroad tracks, way behind the liquor store and gun store, living as far from the nice houses and nice people without actually being outside Marietta's city limits proper.

Amanda didn't want to know the family history. It was painful, brutal. The Scrantons didn't really work anywhere. There was no career path, no steady respectable employment, no upward mobility in any size, shape or form. Instead they survived by doing this and that, eating this and that, dressing in this and that. They were what no one wanted to be.

No wonder Lt. Colonel Don Justice didn't want his only

son dating Julie Scranton. It must have made his skin crawl. It made her skin crawl just thinking about it now. Her poor, desperate mother trying to escape the ugliness of her world by falling in love with a handsome boy from the best part of town.

Amanda would never be able to look at Tyler now without remembering the past.

"I don't think this is a good idea," she said hoarsely. "It's not good for either of us—"

"Why?"

"You hate Montana—"

"I don't hate Montana."

"And I love it here. And I always want to live here."

"What does that have to do with you and me?"

"You're only here because Cormac's company is here, and he's bringing you on board. But if he didn't, you'd be out of here so fast."

"You don't know that."

"But neither do you." Her voice broke, and she pressed her lips together to keep them from trembling. "This was never your dream to be locked down in Marietta, and I'm certainly not going to be the one to trap you here, either."

"What if this wasn't a trap, but the place I could see being home? What if I wanted to be here? What then, Mandy?"

Her heart was pounding and her stomach was churning and yet all she could feel was sadness. To think that Don had despised Mandy's mother so much...

It was one thing to have someone like Carol Bingley say *what was right with the Wright girls?*, but to know there were others who'd said the same about her mother was shattering. Was being poor really so awful? Was poverty such a stigma?

Amanda closed her eyes, feeling how they stung and burned. Her chest burned, too. Everything inside of her hurt.

She'd thought she'd put the past in the past. She'd thought that working hard would distance her from the pain and shame, but suddenly the shame was alive and well, and it was burning her up.

It didn't matter that she'd gone to college and earned a bachelor's degree. It didn't matter that she'd worked, and worked, and worked. It didn't matter that she owned her own business now.

"Tonight was the wake-up call we both needed," she said, arms crossed over her chest to keep herself from shivering, which was so weird because she was also on fire, also burning up.

Anger warred with shame. Pain shadowed everything. But beyond the pain was the fierce need to survive.

"There is no wake-up call, Mandy."

"Maybe not for you, but there was for me. This isn't going to work long-term. We're too different—"

"You're just upset, and I get it. Tonight was rough. Shocking. But there's no need to make a knee-jerk reaction."

"Tyler, we were never meant to be, let's just end it here

and now. Let's end it while we can still be friends."

"I don't want to be your friend. I want you to by my girl, my love, my future."

Hot tears scalded her eyes and Amanda went to the door and yanked it open. "I'm sorry. I'm done. I'm out. Please go now."

"I'm not letting you go."

"Don't be like Kirk. Please?"

He flinched, his jaw jutting.

She hardened herself against remorse. She wasn't going to feel, and she wasn't going to care, and most of all, she was done apologizing for who she was, and where she came from. She couldn't help her family history, or her past, and, to be honest, she was proud of everything she'd accomplished considering there hadn't been a lot of parental input or involvement. She liked that everything she'd done had been because she and her sisters had banded together and become their own little tribe... a band of warrior girls. There was nothing wrong with them. They were the Wright sisters. They were right. They were *perfect*.

And if others couldn't see, then that was their problem. Not hers.

"Enjoy your new job. Enjoy your new life here in Marietta," she said, "but it's not going to be with me."

TYLER WALKED BACK to his grandmother's with Amanda's

voice echoing in his head. *Don't be like Kirk.*

The words drummed in his head, whipping his anger, but by the time he reached Gram's house, his anger was replaced by fierce resolve.

He was not going to lose her like this, not over something that had nothing to do with them.

Despite the frigid wind blowing, he turned around and walked back to Amanda's.

He was not going to let her break things off because of something that happened to their parents when they were just teenagers. Admittedly, it wasn't the most comfortable discovery, but their failed relationship thirty-five plus years ago didn't doom his and Mandy's.

He knocked on her door, hard, and then again. He knew she was aware he was outside because he'd sent her a text already saying he was on her doorstep, waiting for her, and she'd answered, telling him she was busy.

I'm not going away, he texted her back.

It's going to be a long night as I'm not coming down, she answered.

At least come to the window.

Why?

I want to talk to you.

We're talking.

No, this is texting. Come to the window.

He waited a long minute, actually many long minutes, but then finally he heard the scrape of wood and he stepped off the porch. One of the tall windows on the second floor scraped open, and Mandy was there, leaning on the sill, face shadowed, her blonde hair pulled up in a high ponytail.

"Hey," he said. "How are you?"

"Very funny."

"No, seriously. How *are* you?"

"Fine. Never been better."

But she wasn't fine. She'd been crying. His chest tightened, tension returning. "Open the door, baby."

"I can't. And I can't do this with you. I need time."

"Time for what?"

"To think, sort things out for myself."

"And what is there to sort out?"

"Who I am, who you are, and why we thought we had something together."

He felt an ache deep in his chest. "Because we had something together, and we still do. If we didn't, you wouldn't be so sad."

"I'm not sad."

"Okay. Fine. Maybe I'm the only one sad, and I am sad, and worried about you, because you matter a lot to me and I hate that something thirty-five years ago is hurting you—"

"It wasn't something thirty-five years ago! It was just a few weeks ago. You thought I was swindling your grandmother. You arrived in town certain I was taking advantage of her—"

"I discovered pretty quickly that that wasn't the case."

"But it's still this thing your family has about being taken advantage of. Funny, my family doesn't have that problem. We've never had that problem. Oh, I know why. It's because we don't have sterling reputations, or anything of value to stain or take."

"Amanda."

"You don't get it. I've grown up with this and I'm over it. I'm so over it, and forgive me, Tyler, but I need to be over you."

"It doesn't have to go this way. You know that, don't you?"

"I don't know that. Unlike you, I don't get to make up my reality. I don't live in an imaginary world of characters and plots. I live in Marietta—"

"Maybe it's time you left Marietta then. Maybe it's time you ventured out and saw the world, going somewhere new—"

"Or maybe the person that doesn't belong in Marietta leaves Marietta." Her voice cracked. "Maybe you need to go." She slammed the window shut and disappeared.

SHE CRIED AFTER he left, cried for lost opportunities and broken dreams, and maybe, broken hearts. She'd fallen for him. Fallen pretty hard. But that didn't necessarily mean they were meant to be. Now she just had to figure out how to stop wanting to see him and being with him.

It wasn't going to be easy because Tyler Justice had taken up residence in her heart, and she could see the future she'd wanted, a future where they married and had babies but it was all a fantasy, just fiction, like those paperback novels stacked on the bookshelf in the living room waiting to be read.

Swiping away tears, she grabbed all of the paperbacks, every last one of them, and ran them out to the garbage and threw them away.

Never again would she read another story about the magic of falling in love. It wasn't real. None of it was.

FOR THE FIRST time that Amanda could remember, she wasn't happy to see Bette walking toward the salon the next morning.

Amanda's hand tightened around the blow dryer, mimicking the knotting in her middle. She didn't want to see Bette, and she didn't want to talk to Bette. Not yet. Not until she'd properly processed everything and sorted through her feelings, including her feelings for Tyler.

Amanda turned off the blow dryer, telling her client that she'd be right back and then exited the salon to catch Bette on the front porch. The last thing she wanted to do was hurt Bette's feelings, but she couldn't handle having her sit in her chair today and make conversation. She needed Bette to give her some time and space.

"Mandy," Bette said, giving her a concerned look. "You're upset. I know you're upset. Please let me fix this."

"There is nothing you can do or fix. There is nothing anyone can do right now but let me try to sort out my feelings. I'm struggling, too."

"Be mad at me, but not Tyler. He's done nothing wrong."

Amanda ground her teeth together. "That may be true, but I'm so very uncomfortable right now. I feel... tricked. Betrayed."

Bette's shoulders sagged. "This is all my fault."

"Can we not do this now?"

"When can we talk then, my dear?"

Amanda looked away, her gaze sweeping the residential street and beyond. "I don't know," she said at length.

Bette's shoulders slumped. "You came out here today, because you didn't want me to come in to the salon."

Amanda struggled with telling her the truth. She struggled to keep control. "I don't think it's good for my clients to hear any of this. It's private. Personal. And I want to keep my personal life out of the salon."

"You want to keep *me* out of the salon."

"I want..." Amanda's chest tightened, and her eyes felt dry and gritty. "I want... time. I need time to figure this out for myself."

"So I shouldn't come to the salon anymore."

Amanda fought back tears. "I think taking a break would

be good for both of us. It doesn't need to be forever. A couple weeks perhaps. Or maybe a month."

"A *month*?"

Bette's crushed expression made it hard for Amanda to breathe. Part of her wanted to give Bette a fierce hug, and another part wanted to run away. She was in so deep with this family. She had too many ties. "Two weeks."

"So I can come back in April?" Bette murmured unsteadily.

Amanda blinked hard, to dry her eyes. "That sounds good. We'll both be feeling better about everything by then."

"I never meant to hurt you, Mandy."

Amanda's tears fell. She furiously brushed them away, one after the other, even as she prayed that none of Carol Bingley's minions were around because then everyone would be saying something horrendous like Amanda Wright got herself pregnant.

"I don't know what I'm feeling. That's the problem. That's why I need time." She struggled to smile but couldn't. "And falling apart makes me feel so much worse. Please let me sort through this my way, okay?"

"Can I give you a hug?"

"Of course."

Amanda hugged Bette back, fresh tears welling. And then Bette was carefully walking down the front steps and heading back to her car and Amanda returned to her station in the salon to finish the blow out for her client. But between her next clients, she told Emily to cancel her appointments for tomorrow, and the rest of the week, and to be on the safe side, the week after that as well. She was going to take a break from Marietta. She needed to leave town. Marietta was too small for her and the Justice family.

IT TOOK AMANDA four and a half hours to reach the Sheenan's cabin overlooking Flathead Lake, and she'd cried for probably two hours of that drive, not straight, obviously, but off and on, especially when certain songs came on the radio and then she'd think of Tyler and the trickle of tears would start again.

She finally turned off the radio and drove in silence, the windows down to allow the bracing March air to swirl in and out of the car, the cold chilling her, making her shiver, but at least freezing the tears in their tracks.

She was not going to think of him.

She was not.

Her fingers flexed against the steering wheel as she approached Polson, and then Sweetheart and then, at last, Cherry Lake. The little town of Cherry Lake was the perfect place to go as the summer tourists wouldn't descend on Flathead Lake for another couple of months, and the orchards of cherry trees weren't yet in bloom, which meant it was only locals in the sleepy little towns dotting the beautiful blue lake.

A number of Marietta residents had family that lived in Polson, Cherry Lake, Sweetheart or Kalispell, while others, like the Sheenans, had a vacation cabin in Mission Mountains, but the Wright family didn't have any connection to the area. She was grateful Trey and McKenna offered the family cabin to her when she asked if it was available for a few days. She supposed she could have booked herself into a B&B or small hotel, but she really wanted solitude and the Sheenan cabin fit the bill.

Parking in front of the split log house, she looked up at the old-fashioned log cabin. It wasn't very big, and it wasn't fancy, but it had a simple, welcoming façade and a lovely stone chimney and she couldn't wait to open up the shutters and build a fire and begin reading the thick literary novel she'd had on her shelf for two years but hadn't yet opened. The book had one of those dark, murky covers and promised a "powerful, unnerving examination of current society," which sounded thoroughly depressing, and honestly suited her just fine. As long as it wasn't a love story, she'd enjoy it.

After unlocking the cabin and opening the windows and front door to air it out, Amanda made up the bed in the master bedroom, fluffed the beautiful antique quilt, and took stock of the supplies in the kitchen. The cabin had been used a few weeks ago, and still had the basics, but she'd need perishables like bread, milk, and eggs. After jotting down a list of supplies she'd want to pick up in town, she climbed back into her car and drove into Cherry Lake.

She poked around downtown, peeking into some of the stores, and window-shopping in others. It was a cute little town, and she made a mental note to return to visit one of the art galleries, before heading to the market to buy her groceries and pick up firewood.

She was back to the cabin within an hour, and unloading the groceries from the trunk of her car, she paused to listen to the twitter of the birds above her, and breathe in the fresh scent of pine. She'd never been one of those kids that went away to camp, and her parents hadn't enjoyed car trips, either, but living so close to Paradise Valley and Yellowstone meant that she'd grown up with mountains and big trees and beautiful rivers in her backyard, and there was something infinitely good and comforting in being here now.

For a moment she imagined Tyler here with her, and it made her feel terribly wistful and teary, and the sorrow was like a hollow thing inside of her. She didn't know how she'd ever survive living in a small town so close to him, but not with him. It was inevitable, too, that she'd spot him places, and people would mention him and he'd be near, but always just out of reach. The idea of seeing him, but not being his… the idea of seeing him with someone else, someone not her, made her want to throw up.

Amanda ruthlessly suppressed all thoughts of him, knowing she'd start crying again, just as she'd cried most of the drive to here, and she couldn't do that, not so soon, not when she was so worn out. Besides, she'd come to Cherry

Lake to escape him, not think of him, and she needed to remember that.

But as the days passed, Amanda found herself checking her phone, somewhat surprised that Tyler hadn't texted or tried to call.

She'd rather thought he might.

She'd imagined he would. And then she'd imagined herself ruthlessly deleting his voicemails and texts. She'd imagined how good she'd feel ignoring him.

But he didn't try to reach out to her, at all.

By Wednesday, Amanda was going stir crazy by herself in the cabin. The book she'd brought was beyond depressing and she missed conversation... but not just with anyone. She missed talking to Tyler.

And she missed Bette.

They weren't just her friends. They'd come to feel like family. Her family. Her people.

On Thursday, when she was certain her phone would never ring again, she got a call from Charity.

"Bette fell." Charity's voice carried over the line, crisp and no nonsense. "She was taken to the ER and, fortunately, she didn't break anything, but it was a hard fall, though—"

"When did it happen?"

"Last night. Leaving your salon."

"*What?* Why didn't anyone call me?"

"I only just found out. And I wasn't supposed to tell you. Tyler and Bette made me swear not to tell you. They didn't want to upset you—"

"How? How did it happen?"

"Bette lost her footing going down the steps and fell hard."

Amanda had to sit, her legs no longer strong enough to support her. "Oh, no."

"She's going to be alright. They wanted to keep her for a night for observation but she wasn't having it, so she's home and Tyler is keeping a close eye on her—"

"This isn't okay."

"The good news is that I don't think you're liable."

"Charity! I'm not worrying about liability. I'm worrying about her." Amanda's voice broke. "This is just terrible. Poor Bette!" She sniffled, heartsick. "I'm coming home. I have to see her."

AMANDA WAS NERVOUS when she knocked on the door of Bette's house. She wasn't sure what she would say to Tyler. For that matter she wasn't sure what she would say to Bette, although facing Bette at this point seemed much easier than Tyler.

She didn't have long to worry, though, because suddenly the gray-green door was swinging open and Tyler stood in the shadowy entry, big shoulders filling the doorway, expression impossible to read.

"You should have told me about your grandmother's

fall," she said, her voice shaking. "You should have been the one to reach out and tell me, not Charity."

"You said you didn't want anything to do with me, *and* you told my grandmother you didn't want to see her for two weeks."

"I meant at the salon, while I try to sort out my feelings. But I wasn't ending our friendship. Bette's been in my life for nine years and I'm not someone who just slams the door in someone's face."

"Huh. I find that surprising."

Amanda ignored the last part. "How is she?"

"Bruised and battered, but she's retained her sense of humor, so that is something."

"Can I see her?"

"Are you going to be nice to her?"

"I'm *always* nice to her, even when I'm upset I'm still nice to her." She glared up at him. "You're the one that I wasn't nice to."

"And why is that?"

Her lips compressed. She glanced away. "I think you know why."

"I get that you are surprised, and hurt, but you made it personal."

She balled her into fists inside her coat pockets. "I was scared. I felt exposed, and ashamed. I... wanted to run away." Her voice thickened. "I don't want anyone around me when I'm hurt. I don't want people to know that I hurt.

It's how I've always protected myself. Wear armor, smile big, and don't let anyone know how sensitive I am underneath."

"Do you wear armor?"

Her lips twisted. She gestured to her hair and then her coat. "This, all of this, is protection. The retro hairstyles, the vintage clothing, this is an Amanda that I created for everyone here in Marietta. It's my you-can't-hurt-me persona, and it usually works."

"Your armor didn't work last week, did it?"

"Nope. Failed big time." She swallowed around the lump in her throat, and blinked, trying to keep her eyes from stinging. "I think I came to dinner that night without it. Apparently, I came as myself, and it wasn't enough." Her voice broke and tears filled her eyes. She reached up to swiftly wipe them away before they could fall. "I'm sorry I said hurtful things to you. I'm sorry I hurt Bette—"

"Gram is fine."

She kept wiping away tears. "She's not fine. She's hurt. She fell leaving my salon. This is terrible, and all my fault—"

He pulled her into him, his arms wrapping around her, holding her against him. "You're not responsible for her fall. And as you'll see in a moment, she really is doing well."

"But you're here, not at work, and isn't this the first week of the new job?"

"We pushed back my start date for a month. Cormac is still finalizing paperwork with TexTron and I've got a project I'm working on, so it's all good. Now come see

Gram, and no more tears, or she'll get weepy, too, and I can handle one emotional woman, but not two."

She gave him a watery smile and drew a deep breath as she approached Bette's bedroom. Tyler hung back in the front part of the house, and she was grateful for that. It was hard enough apologizing without having an audience.

She knocked lightly on the door and then pushed it open. Bette was sitting up in bed, wearing one of her cute bed robes, and doing a crossword puzzle on a white wicker bed table.

"Hi, Bette. It's me. Can I come in?" Amanda said nervously.

"Oh, yes, dear, of course." Bette gestured for her to enter, her hand a knobby purple black. "You have the best timing, too. What is an eight letter word for a hairstylist that begins with 'c'?"

With Bette's head down, she hadn't seen the bruises or swelling, but now that Bette was looking up at her, the black eye, split lip, and swollen jaw was very much in evidence.

Amanda crossed quickly to her side. "Oh, Bette, you look like you went twelve rounds in the boxing ring."

"If only that were the case. Instead I tumbled down stairs. Silly me. I much prefer the idea of being bloodied through proper sport."

Amanda snorted, and sat down on the side of the bed. "I understand you refused to stay overnight at the hospital."

"Nothing's broken, and hospitals are such miserable

places. I'm better off here where I have some peace and quiet." Bette tapped the crossroad with her pencil. "I've been stuck on this one for far too long. Hoping you can help me? I need an eight letter word for a hairstylist, and it begins with 'c.'"

"Coiffeur," Amanda answered promptly.

Bette filled in the letters before looking up at her, surprised. "Yes! How did you know? Do you use that word in your work?"

"No. But the word was used on *Jeopardy* once and I've never forgotten." Amanda lightly covered Bette's wrist, careful to avoid all bruises. "I am so sorry—"

"No, my girl. I'm sorry. I'm a terrible coward and I should have told you long ago about your mother and Patrick, and how I always cared for her, and worried about her, even years after she'd married your father and had you children. I know Julie was hurt by everything that happened, and I never forgave myself for not standing up to Don. Your mother deserved better. Patrick deserved better. I wish I had a good excuse as to why I didn't do more. I suppose my only defense is, in those days, wives didn't challenge their husbands. At least military wives didn't. I hope things are different now."

Amanda glanced down at the crossword puzzle that was now completed. Funny how the only word missing was coiffeur, or stylist. She exhaled and said as lightly as she could, "If my mother hadn't married my father, I wouldn't be here."

"And what a loss that would be. You are a joy, and a light, and you have brought me such happiness, Amanda. I know I'm not your mother, or your grandmother, but I love you as if you were my own."

Amanda blinked hard, chasing away the threat of tears. "Please don't make me cry. I feel like all I've done the past few days is cry. I'm ready to start smiling and feeling like me again."

"Me, too," Bette agreed, before hesitating. "Have you and Tyler sorted everything out between the two of you?"

"Not everything, not yet."

"Then what are you doing in here? Get out of here. Have a good talk. He's been very worried about you."

Amanda rose. "I will, but I've a question. I've been wondering about this and I thought maybe I should just ask. Tyler told me that you'd called yourself my business partner, and I figured you meant it as in being my biggest cheerleader, but do you really want to go into business with me? Are you wanting to be my real partner?"

Bette blushed. "Oh, no, not a real partner, not with responsibilities and duties, no. But I do love to get excited about your projects, because you truly do have the best ideas."

"So do you." Amanda leaned over and kissed Bette lightly on the cheek, before adding with a smile, "Because I figured out why you told Tyler that you'd made several sizable gifts to me. You wanted to get his attention. You wanted to get him to Marietta. And you wanted him to meet me. Am I right?"

Bette smiled a self-satisfied smile. "And you said no matchmaking."

"And you ignored me."

"Because I knew better. I knew you two would be perfect for each other and I was right."

After saying goodbye to Bette, Amanda went in search of Tyler and found him outside, in the front of the house, talking to Charity. Neither of them heard her approach, and from their expressions, they looked serious.

"Is everything okay?" Amanda asked glancing from one to the other.

"Yes," Charity answered quickly. "I was just talking to Tyler about something I was working on, wanting his input. He's great with design. Must be all those years of studying graphic design." She reached into her coat pocket and pulled out her keys. "I was sent to find you. Mom wants to talk to you. I'm to drive you over to the house."

"I can drive myself, but I'd love to go home first and shower and change—"

"Nope. Mom wants to talk now. Dad's out and she thought this is the best time."

Amanda's brow furrowed. Charity's voice sounded a little too high and her tone a little too bright. "Are Mom and Dad okay?"

"They're fine. Come on. Get in. I want to get this over with as I'm trying to hit the six o'clock mat Pilates class at the gym."

"That's two hours from now. You'll make it." Amanda crossed to Tyler, and put a hand on his sleeve. "Am I welcome to return later?"

"Do you want to return later?" he countered.

She nodded.

He kissed her. "Then, absolutely."

AS CHARITY PARKED in front of the blue house, Amanda sucked in a breath, bracing herself for whatever was to come. It was never an easy thing returning to their childhood home on Chance Avenue. Growing up, "home" was anything but a refuge. No, life in their house was consistently chaotic. Even in high school she'd dreaded walking through the front door, never sure what she would find. If her father had been drinking, there would be yelling and fighting, or if she'd arrived after the drinking, her father would be snoring in front of the TV while her mother cried in the kitchen, or the bedroom.

She and Charity used to comfort themselves that it could be worse.

Dad could hit Mom—but he didn't.

Mom could hook up with strange men—but she didn't.

And didn't everyone have dysfunction in their family

somewhere?

Charity removed the key from the ignition. "Things really are better," she said, as if able to read her sister's mind. "They're both trying. Dad's at an AA meeting now."

"That's good."

"And they've cut up their credit cards so Dad can't do his online shopping."

"That's even better."

They both looked at the weathered blue house with the sagging front porch. "I wish Dad would paint it," Amanda said. "Or maybe we just come and paint it for them. Make it a Mother's Day-Father's Day gift."

"What would Chance Avenue be without our blue house? It's legendary," Charity said mockingly, aware that it was well-known for all the wrong reasons. It hadn't been blue when their parents bought the house, either. Dad had painted it when the girls were little. He used to say he painted it blue because he needed something manly to come home to, since he lived in a house full of women. Amanda had believed him, and it wasn't until a few years ago she discovered he'd painted it blue because the local mercantile had mixed up 15 gallons of Smurf blue by mistake, and instead of throwing it out, the store manager gave it to her father for their house.

"No wonder I live in a pink house. It's my response to being forced to grow up in a blue one," Amanda said, opening her door. "Come on. Let's get this over with."

While Charity watched TV in the living room, Julie led Amanda to her bedroom and closed the door.

"I want to show you something," Julie said, bringing out a small box from the back of her top dresser drawer. It wasn't a very fancy box, but a faded baby-blue cardboard, the small square lid creased, as if it had been accidentally flattened. Inside the box was a small gray silk pouch. Julie handed Amanda the silk pouch.

Amanda looked questioningly at her mom.

"My promise ring," her mom said tightly, flatly, no expression in her eyes or voice.

"Wait. *What?*"

"It's my ring, the one Patrick gave me."

"He gave you a ring?"

"Yes."

"Why?"

"He loved me."

Amanda's hand shook slightly as she dumped the delicate pearl ring into the palm of her hand. She turned the ring over, examining it in the light. "He gave this to you before he left for college?"

"No. He sent it from college, just before Christmas his sophomore year."

"But you two broke up before the end of his senior year."

"No, we didn't. We kept seeing each other. Just in secret."

Amanda struggled to take it all in. This isn't the story

she'd been told. "Bette said Don split you two up. She said—"

"Oh, Mr. Justice tried to, and he was angry, and very unpleasant, but Patrick wasn't intimidated. You couldn't threaten him. He stood up for the underdog, always. He was quite fearless, actually, and it's why I fell in love with him. Bette might think Patrick walked away from me, but it didn't happen. There was no way he was going to let anyone—much less his father—come between us."

"So he didn't forget you right away?"

"He *never* forgot me." Julie blinked, lashes suddenly damp. "I blew him off."

"*What?*"

"I met your dad, and we um… I… got pregnant, and so I called Patrick and told him I was marrying someone else, and that was that."

"You were pregnant with Jenny before you married?"

"That shocks you?"

"I didn't know."

"She was a very small baby, and so we told everyone she was born early."

Amanda turned the ring over, her head spinning. "Why didn't you give the ring back to Patrick?"

"I tried. He didn't want it. He said it was for me, and he wanted me to keep it as a thank-you for taking a chance on him." Julie drew a slow breath, fresh tears filling her eyes. "He thanked *me* for taking a chance on him. Crazy. I had nothing, and he had everything, and yet he still wanted me, and he'd waited for me, for years he waited for me, but in the end, I couldn't wait. I didn't like being alone. So when I met your dad, and he was here, and available, I... moved on."

Amanda's fingers curled around the ring as she sat down on the trunk at the foot of the bed. "I don't know what to say."

"I've never discussed any of this, because what's the point? But when Charity told me that you'd broken up with Tyler, and you'd told Bette to stay away from the salon, I knew we had to talk. Mandy, if Tyler is anything like Patrick, he's a *good* man. Loyal, loving, honorable. Don't judge him harshly because of me, and don't run away from a chance at true happiness. Patrick didn't fail me, Mandy. I failed him."

Amanda's head thumped. "Does Dad know about Patrick?"

"He knows there was a high school boyfriend who'd given me a promise ring."

"Have you shown him the ring?"

"He found it once in the back of my lingerie drawer."

"And he doesn't mind that you kept it?"

"He doesn't feel threatened by a ring."

Amanda could feel the weight of the past in the room and a dozen different things came to her mind, things she'd love to ask, things she'd love to know, but her mother's expression was strained and pressing her mom for details and more information didn't seem fair. "That's good," she said softly, sliding the ring back into the gray silk pouch. "I'm glad."

But her mother didn't seem to feel any better. She kept blinking back tears. "I love your dad."

"I know you do."

"And I've always been loyal to him, even during the hard years, and there have been plenty of hard years. But after breaking Patrick's heart, I vowed I'd never do that again. And so I've stood by your dad through thick and thin."

"Mom, I'm not judging you."

"But has it been easy? No. Did I love Patrick? Yes. Would my life have been different if I'd been more patient and willing to wait for him? Absolutely. But we make choices and I made mine." She hesitated. "Don't make the same mistakes I did."

Amanda held the silk pouch out for her mom to take but Julie shook her head. "I don't want it. You keep it."

"And what would I do with it?"

"Maybe give it to Tyler. Or Bette. What do you think?"

Amanda closed her fingers around the pouch, holding it secure in her palm. "I think it's time our families had some closure and moved on."

CHAPTER ELEVEN

THE PLAN HAD been for Charity to drop Amanda off at Bette's and head to the gym. It was after five and the sun was dropping lower in the sky, long golden rays of sunlight piercing the bare branches of trees on Bramble and streaming across the asphalt.

Amanda squinted against the light as Charity neared Bette's house. Something huge and pink filled Bette's driveway.

And then she let out a scream.

It was an RV. A shocking pink RV. Not a soft pink pastel or a wash of pink. No, this was almost Pepto pink; this was the pink of her house and salon.

Charity pulled up in front of the house and Amanda read the script on the side of the RV, *The Wright Mobile Salon*, painted in purple.

She read it again even as she jumped out of the car, thinking the purple script was fun and bold, and very sassy.

She rushed toward the RV. Tyler was sitting in the vehicle's open doorway, waiting for her, and he stood up as she neared him.

"Wow," she murmured, a lump in her throat. It was her

pink, her name, her dream... her mobile salon. She crossed her arms tightly over her chest, not wanting him to see that she was shaking. "But this isn't my RV. Mine is still parked behind my house."

"It is a different one," he agreed.

She frowned, confused.

He crossed the patch of grass separating them. "Gram's needed too much work. Everything needed to be overhauled, and even then, I had serious concerns about safety. I wasn't about to have you on the road in rough weather, in a vehicle that was pretty, but unreliable. Ultimately it just made more sense to find something newer, with fewer miles, so it'd be in better condition."

"But that meant you had to buy something, whereas Bette's was already paid for."

"The repairs to Gram's would have been substantial."

"And yet I loved the idea of driving Bette's RV."

"But Gram never drove it. My grandfather did." His mouth tightened, jaw firming. "And I'm all for good memories, but I've always struggled with my grandfather's hard stance on people and priorities. He alienated my father. He was critical of his grandsons. The whole reason Coby joined the military was to make him proud, and yet when Coby died, my grandfather couldn't find any words to comfort my mother or father." He grimaced. "I love Gram, but you don't need her old RV, and thankfully, Gram agreed with me."

Amanda turned back to the pink RV, overwhelmed. She

blinked back tears, and fought the tightness in his throat that was preventing her from speaking. All she could think about was the pearl ring in her pocket, and the discovery that Patrick had loved her mom, and had never abandoned her, and now here was Tyler trying to give her her dream.

"You don't like it," he said.

"No. That's not... that's not what I'm feeling. It's that I'm not sure what to say." Her jaw worked, the lump in her throat seemed to grow bigger, making it painful to speak. "I didn't want you to do this for me. I wanted to do it myself, when I could afford to—"

"Gram said it would hurt your pride. Seems she was right."

"This isn't about my pride."

"Of course it's about your pride. It's your Achilles' heel."

"What does that mean?"

"In story terms, every hero has an Achilles' heel, and that Achilles' heel is what makes the hero great, but it's what will ultimately bring him or her down."

"You're saying my pride is my downfall."

He looked at her, brow lifted. He was so incredibly annoying.

"You're wrong," she said tightly.

"It wouldn't be the first time," he said cheerfully. "We all have flaws and faults. And for your information, I never expected you to be perfect—"

"Because you didn't expect anything from me at all, or at

least, nothing good."

"No, what I discovered is that you're surprisingly perfect. Even with your pride." His expression was tender, and amused. "Mandy, baby, I love you. You're not just everything to me, you're home. You're my world. Wherever you are, it's where I want to be."

A shiver shot through her, making her legs feel weak. He didn't mean that, did he? Was he even aware of what he was saying? She slid her hand into her pocket and desperately clasped the silk pouch, holding it so tightly that the pearl dug into her skin. "For now, you mean."

"No. Forever." He reached for her, and drew her to him, ignoring her resistance. "Maybe you didn't catch what I said, so I'll say it more slowly. I. Love. You." He was smiling down at her, and yet his voice was deep and a little hoarse. "You are home. Wherever you are, it's where I want to be."

"Even if it's on the road, in this pink RV?"

His finger stroked her cheek. "Even if it's living together in this pink RV." And then his head dipped, and he kissed her lightly, before murmuring, "But maybe we don't actually live in the RV? We removed the bed to make room for your shampoo bowls and salon chairs and there would be nowhere to sleep."

She laughed, and kissed him. He was awfully irresistible. "Tell me the chairs are pink."

"Of course they are. What other color could they possibly be?"

She laughed again, and as she looked up into his face, his rugged, beautiful face with the gorgeous green eyes and movie star smile, she thought he might be as handsome as a romance cover hero, but he was *better*, because he was real, and he was hers.

"I love you, Tyler James Justice," she whispered. "Probably far more than I should."

"There is no such thing as too much love."

And then he kissing her again, the slow, deep bone-melting kisses he was so very good at, the kind that made her forget she didn't want or need a man, because honestly, why couldn't she be a successful, independent woman, who'd found a successful, independent man? Wasn't that really the best of both worlds?

"Does this mean she said yes?" a thin voice quavered from the front porch.

Amanda and Tyler broke apart, both moving to the porch at the same time.

"Gram!"

"Bette."

"Well?" She was leaning on a cane, still dressed in her bed robe and pajamas. "Nobody was telling me anything and I couldn't wait any longer. Does she like the RV?"

"Yes," Amanda answered, climbing the steps and putting a hand on Bette's elbow to make sure she was steady. Tyler moved to the other side, neither wanting to risk her taking another fall.

Bette glanced from one to the other. "And did she say she'd marry you, Ty?"

Color darkened his cheekbones. "Gram," he muttered, with a shake of his head. "Not now."

"What do you mean, not now? Did she say no?"

"Gram, I haven't asked her yet."

"Well, ask her. We don't want to lose her. She's a keeper, Tyler."

"I know, Gram. I've told her." Still shaking his head he looked at Amanda over the top of his grandmother's head. "This isn't the romantic proposal I'd imagined, but it couldn't be more heartfelt—"

"Wait. Not like that," Bette interrupted. "You have to kneel. You can't propose standing up—"

"Yes, he can," Amanda interrupted, putting her hand out to stop him from getting down on one knee. "And, yes, the answer is yes, yes, yes!"

CHAPTER TWELVE

THEY ENDED UP holding the wedding the first Saturday of June at the Emerson Barn, the place they had their first dance and their first kiss. Perhaps they hadn't fallen in love with each other that night, but it had been a magical evening, and when they were trying to pick a place to hold the ceremony and reception the only place that came to mind was the big handsome barn in Paradise Valley.

Amanda's only real concern about the venue was its size. It was huge. Cavernous without all the tables and chairs, and they both came from small families. How would they ever fill it?

Bette brushed aside Mandy's concerns because there were lots of ways to make the space look more intimate through trellises and flowers, chandeliers and screens.

Bette ended up playing a bigger role in the planning of the wedding than expected, but Amanda didn't mind, not when Bette was so excited. It had been her dream forever, to have her beloved grandson fall in love with her Mandy. With the wedding just two months out, they divided up the tasks so that not all the planning fell onto Mandy's shoulders.

Amanda would be in charge of the ceremony and finding the right gown, bridesmaid dresses, flowers, and choosing the invitation. Tyler was responsible for the reception, organizing dinner, music for dancing, and making the space less overwhelming. Bette said she'd oversee the mailing of the invitations as she knew of an excellent local calligrapher who'd address the invitations, and she'd have the responses come back to her and keep track of the replies so Mandy would have one less thing to do since it wasn't good for brides to be stressed out.

Amanda asked Charity to be her maid of honor, and Charity embraced her responsibilities with zeal, as organizing people and things was her particular specialty, and since organizing was her strength, she told Mandy she wanted to make her wedding dress but it would be a surprise. She wasn't going to tell her what it looked like, only that it would be beautiful and perfect and it'd fit her like a glove. Amanda was delighted. Because what could be better than having her talented sister, who was also her best friend, design a custom gown for her?

Late April, Jenny flew in from Colorado and the three sisters, their mom, and Sadie and Tricia went shopping together for the mother of the bride dress and the four bridesmaid dresses at Married in Marietta. Lisa Renee, the store owner, helped them personally, and it was clear that Charity had already tipped Lisa off on the types of bridesmaid dresses she thought would be perfect for the wedding, and had a variety of pink gowns that were decidedly romantic. Some were a flirty cocktail length, while others were long, but they all were fitted through the waist with full pretty skirts.

There were so many lovely options, and the girls tried on a number of styles, and any of them would work, she just wanted her friends and sisters comfortable, but the fact that Mandy didn't love any of them didn't sit well with Charity and so she whispered something to Lisa, and Lisa disappeared into the back and then returned with a stunning, strapless ballerina-style gown, featuring an icy-blue silk satin bodice with a full white tulle skirt over a blue silk satin underskirt, and gorgeous hand-stitched pink flowers across the ice-blue bodice's neckline.

Amanda's eyes widened. It was the most perfect thing she'd ever seen. "This is so beautiful. It's just stunning." She looked at Charity. "Would you mind trying it on?"

Charity returned a few minutes later in the dress and it was the dress—exactly what Mandy wanted for her bridesmaids—and yet the dress couldn't be inexpensive, not when it looked like couture. "How much is this one?" she asked.

"Not as much as you'd think. They're from a winter formal collection, and then your sister and Sadie made a few modifications, adding the flowers, and the layers of tulle."

Amanda looked to Charity and Sadie and they were both grinning. "We knew you'd love this one," Sadie confessed. "But we didn't want you to see it until you'd looked at a lot of other dresses first because we really did want you to feel like you had options."

"So you'd still need to modify three more dresses?" Amanda asked, worried about the work involved.

"It's not a big deal, and I'm going to do the bridesmaid dresses," Sadie answered, "because Charity is doing your bridal gown."

Amanda couldn't stop smiling. "I love it. Let's do it."

AMANDA WOKE EARLY on the morning of their wedding day, and she went for a run to help burn off some of her nervous energy. For the past nine years, she'd helped dozens and dozens of brides get ready for their big day, and she'd never understood why they were so anxious, but this morning she felt emotional and almost jittery.

Back home, she took a long bath before heading downstairs just in time to greet Bette, and her mother, and her bridesmaids, who'd all arrived for their hair appointments.

Tricia opened a bottle of champagne, and the girls all sipped champagne while her mother's hair was drawn into a pretty, relaxed chignon with wisps of hair drawn loose to frame the face. And then it was Mandy's turn, but because she still didn't know what her dress looked like, Charity directed the stylist to give Amanda a "Grace Kelly updo"— clean, classic, and elegant.

And then it was time to dress, and because the salon was

closed today to outside business since all of the stylists had been invited to the late afternoon wedding, the girls were able to take over the upstairs and downstairs of the house. Upstairs, Charity finally revealed Amanda's bridal gown. It was without a doubt an ode to the 1950s with its long fitted sheer lace sleeves, and lace bodice over a strapless heart-shaped corset. The full tulle ball gown skirt featured a wildly romantic lace apron, with layer upon layer of lace, as if a waterfall. The waist was narrow, the lace neckline almost severe across her shoulders, and yet the generous lace apron, was whimsical and fun.

"Just like you," Charity whispered in Amanda's ear, giving her a fierce hug.

Amanda's stiff tulle veil stopped just short of her elbows, and was topped with a crown of white flowers that Sadie had created.

Amanda had planned to wear simple diamond stud earrings but Jenny pulled out a velvet jewelry box. "For your something old, something new, something borrowed, something blue. We've covered it all. Old, new, borrowed, blue."

Opening the box Amanda discovered a pair of pearl earrings surrounded by a cluster of diamonds and a single sapphire.

"We matched the pearl Tyler's dad gave Mom," Jenny said, "and then we all chipped in and had them reset with a few sparkly stones."

"The sapphire in each was a gift from Bette," Charity added.

"We thought it was a way to incorporate the past, and the future," Amanda's mom said quietly. "What do you think?"

"I love them," Amanda answered huskily, hugging each of her friends and family. "It's wonderful. You're all so wonderful, and I'm so very grateful for each of you. Thank you for being here today and thank you for making me feel so special."

There were tearful hugs all the way around and then it was time to pack up and head to the Emerson Barn for the late afternoon ceremony and as Amanda climbed into the limousine waiting out front, she said a little prayer of gratitude for all the blessings in her life. What a truly lovely, magical day.

As the limousine approached Emerson Barn, Amanda thought she knew all the surprises, but as she entered the barn, she discovered that the cavernous space had been transformed by dozens and dozens of trees wrapped in tiny pink fairy lights. The entire barn glowed pink, and there at the front, before the big arched window, stood Tyler and his groomsmen.

Once she spotted Tyler, she couldn't look away. He was so handsome and dashing in his tuxedo. She felt almost dizzy with joy.

She heard the strains of music, and it was time for the

bridesmaids to go, and then soon it would be her turn. She took her dad's arm, and gave him a kiss, and then an encouraging squeeze.

He patted her hand. "Enjoy today, Mandy."

She nodded, and blinked back tears, happy tears. "Oh, I will. I absolutely will."

EPILOGUE

TYLER AND AMANDA'S first daughter was born in the middle of a brutal Montana snowstorm. Thankfully, the hospital was a relatively short drive from their home on Bramble, and Tyler had become adept at driving in harsh Montana weather so the blinding snow was an inconvenience more than anything.

Labor progressed quickly, so quickly that Elizabeth Marie Justice was born shortly after midnight, after just four hours of labor. Baby Elizabeth was named after her beloved great-grandmother, Elizabeth 'Bette' Marie Justice, and there was no better great-grandmother in the world than Gram.

Amanda's business flourished, and Tyler came to love Marietta as much as his wife. And Amanda never stopped counting her blessings, because her brilliant, perceptive, loving husband had taught her that dreams really do come true.

THE END

Love on Chance Avenue Series

Book 1: *Take Me, Cowboy*
Winner of the RITA® Award for Best Romance Novella

Book 2: *Miracle on Chance Avenue*

Book 3: *Take a Chance on Me*

Available now at your favorite online retailer!

THE TAMING OF THE SHEENANS

The Sheenans are six powerful wealthy brothers from Marietta, Montana. They are big, tough, rugged men, and as different as the Montana landscape.

Christmas at Copper Mountain
Book 1: Brock Sheenan's story

Tycoon's Kiss
Book 2: Troy Sheenan's story

The Kidnapped Christmas Bride
Book 3: Trey Sheenan's story

Taming of the Bachelor
Book 4: Dillion Sheenan's story

A Christmas Miracle for Daisy
Book 5: Cormac Sheenan's story

The Lost Sheenan's Bride
Book 6: Shane Sheenan's story

Available now at your favorite online retailer!

ABOUT THE AUTHOR

New York Times and USA Today bestselling author of over fifty five romances and women's fiction titles, **Jane Porter** has been a finalist for the prestigious RITA award five times and won in 2014 for Best Novella with her story, Take Me, Cowboy, from Tule Publishing. Today, Jane has over 12 million copies in print, including her wildly successful, Flirting With Forty, picked by Redbook as its Red Hot Summer Read, and reprinted six times in seven weeks before being made into a Lifetime movie starring Heather Locklear. A mother of three sons, Jane holds an MA in Writing from the University of San Francisco and makes her home in sunny San Clemente, CA with her surfer husband and two dogs.

Thank you for reading

Take a Chance on Me

If you enjoyed this book, you can find more from all our great authors at TulePublishing.com, or from your favorite online retailer.

TULE
PUBLISHING